Those Benignant Eyes

Darren John Wilson

First Edition Published in the United Kingdom
in 2024 by aSys Publishing

eBook Edition First Published in the United Kingdom
in 2024 by aSys Publishing

Disclaimer

This is a work of fiction. Names, characters, businesses, places, events and incidents are either the products of the author's imagination or used in a fictitious manner. Any resemblance to actual persons, living or dead, or actual events is purely coincidental.

ISBN: 978-1-913438-82-1
aSys Publishing 2024

CONTENTS

Double Vision

Fifteen years ago, when I was a young man of twenty—barely a man at all, it might be argued—I used to frequent a pub that was so popular with people only just old enough to drink that anyone there over thirty years of age was considered geriatric. One such relic was Sandra. At thirty-five, she was practically a fossil.

Not much was known about Sandra, so she was not much talked about, and, because she was not much talked about, not much was known about her. To talk about her would have been to acknowledge her presence, and her presence was unsettling, like a tramp's at a society garden party, or a troll's at a beauty pageant. There was nothing out of the ordinary to distinguish her from any other peroxide-blonde of her age and class. But that was just her appearance. It was her demeanour that was odd and that unsettled people around her. It was that from which the regulars at the Square and Compass recoiled. She was a solitary woman, incongruous in the midst of people considerably younger than herself, and she floated around the always-busy public house without so much as a word spoken, simply smiling at people, ghostlike, more solid than an apparition but less substantial than the human, like a cloud of smoke that one could reach out and touch, and not only touch, but clutch, and hold onto, and then let go of, as one pleased.

Though my friends and I thought her strange, we indulged her, mindful that any one of us, should life take a turn for the worse, might be her some fifteen years hence. Something had broken her. We could tell that much. But we did not need to know what that something was. Nor did we want to know. Perhaps she would mend, we thought, or she might break further. We were mature enough to speculate, but too young to understand. We treated her as part of the furniture at the Square and Compass, a moveable extension of the tables and chairs, a fixture as much as a fitting; a haunting visitation; an emanation of something best kept hidden, something, though essentially harmless, both hideous and repulsive. Many of us saw in her a warning of what might become of us. Life for us was only just beginning, but life might yet take us in its grip and spoil us, ruin us even, and upon that possibility we chose not to dwell for longer than it took to swallow a mouthful of our favourite tipple.

One evening, the unthinkable happened. Sandra spoke to one of us. She spoke to *me*. Then one thing led to another. What possessed her to drift across the pub in her character-istically ethereal manner towards me, I cannot say. Our eyes had not met across the crowded, smoke-filled room. If they had then that recollection has escaped me. She took me com-pletely by surprise. To this day, I cannot explain why I did what I did. Nothing like it had ever happened before, and nothing like it has happened since. It was as if I had sum-moned her and she had answered my call and was standing there patiently awaiting an explanation. I remember feeling strangely alone and vulnerable in her company when, before she appeared out of the blue, I had felt a little awkward (as was normal for me in society) but still part of the crowd. I was bonded to her now in a way that nobody else present had ever been, or ever would be, and that unsettled me greatly. Like an impala being hunted by a lion, I had been separated from the crowd. The thought that she and I might be kindred spirits, drawn to each other in some way as life crashed and burned around us, scared me half to death as I stood there wondering what on earth I should say.

In the blink of an eye, I became aware of just how pretty Sandra was, even with a cigarette smouldering between the fingers of her left hand. True, the colour of her hair had been determined by the contents of a bottle, but it looked natural enough, and her skin was smooth as porcelain and her teeth a gleaming white, unaffected, it seemed, by the ravages of nicotine and smoke. She had an enticing shape, too, voluptuous and beautifully curvaceous as she was in tight denim jeans. It is no exaggeration to say that her physical allurements were manifold. I was made to wonder, as I had not wondered before, why she was alone, with no male chaperone, a sad and solitary figure, that night as every night.

We exchanged pleasantries like two people trying to dance *with* each other but succeeding only in dancing *around* each other, and I dare say that I failed to distinguish myself with my conversational opening salvo. Thankfully, my memory has spared me the embarrassment of recollecting that particularly nauseating moment of my life by consigning it to a place from which I cannot retrieve it. The substantive part of our sordid dialogue, alas, has not succeeded in giving my internal cerebral censor the slip.

"I've heard that kissing someone who smokes is like kissing an ashtray."

That is what I said to her. After two years or so spent observing her meanderings around my local pub, they were the first meaningful words that I spoke to her. I wish they had been my last. Even now, fifteen years on, I have no idea what possessed me to utter those vulgar words. Her reply was more vulgar still.

"Would you like to put that to the test?"

We went outside, found somewhere private, and kissed in the rain. Though our encounter gave me—and, I dare say, her—a transgressive thrill, I found myself wishing to withdraw—to recoil—from it no sooner had it begun. The act was shameful: not so much erotic foreplay as the precursor of a coupling that could never have been consummated. My eventual withdrawal was an untidy, awkward affair, with much sighing and adjustment of clothing and rearrangement of facial features. Once I had recovered from the mutual touching of lips, I awaited her damning verdict on my sad little performance, so I was surprised when she asked me for my assessment of her mouth's resemblance to an ashtray.

"You might smoke menthol cigarettes from now on," I suggested.

"Oh," she said, "I've heard that menthol cigarettes are an aphrodisiac."

"I wouldn't know about that," I responded lamely, now keen to be back inside the pub where it was warm and dry and safe.

"We could put *that* claim to the test too," she said.

At that, I tore myself away from her, bundled through the back door, out of the front—making a terrible scene as I went—and never set foot inside that pub again. That, indeed, was my first and last close encounter with a woman. Something about it had disgusted me. I did not like the person I was during those fateful moments. I wanted never to be that person again. I do not blame Sandra. She was merely the catalyst. She summoned the Devil from somewhere deep inside me; and I was determined that he would never get an outing again. He could not. He would not. I resolved never to make myself so vulnerable again, so exposed, and so utterly defenceless. I had to put myself out of harm's way.

What happened to me some fifteen years after that incident had happened to me before, and not infrequently. Many times, then, had I passed somebody in the street and recognised in them—or thought I had—a person from my past, only to see, a few minutes later, someone else and realise that that *was* the person that I thought I had seen moments earlier. I tended to think of the phenomenon as some kind of retrospective premonition. Whenever it happened, I simply shook my head, knowingly, and acknowledged the tricks that my imagination—or my intuition, call it what you will—liked to play on me.

There I was, walking across Trafalgar Square, on my way back from Westminster Palace, where I had been to see a Lord Spiritual, the Anglican Bishop of Winchester, about some ecumenical matter or other that was bound to yield no fruit whatsoever, as if the Established and Catholic Churches were simply going through the motions of trying to find enough common theological ground to improve relations sufficiently even to begin to think about effecting a union. That is when I saw her. That is when I *thought* I saw her. She looked supremely happy, in love, laughing and smiling as she was on the arm of a man, a strong-looking man with chiselled features and a robust physique. She looked prosperous, too, in a black fur coat and a red sequin dress, as if she had just dined in one of the capital's smartest restaurants. Her hair was still a dyed blonde, though she had now assumed the posture of a distinguished middle-aged woman; someone, indeed, whom one might call a lady.

Seeing her was no occasion for wonderment at fate's mischievous machinations, for our town was no more than fifty miles from London and its people were known to travel up to the metropolis to work and to play and even to love. I just thought it odd to see her there when I had not set eyes on her in our town in the fifteen years since our brief encounter. She did not see me, and I made no attempt to catch her attention, or to speak with her. I simply walked by and left her to her happy life. Quietly, to myself, I thanked her for the part she had played in making me who I was. I had found a safe place with the God of my salvation. That was down to her.

As I approached Saint Martin-in-the-Fields, I beheld a commotion outside the church. I had planned to take a peep inside, perhaps even to stay for Choral Evensong. It was that time of the day. How delightful would be the sound of pure English song in the midst of a city where so much was now exotic? The Anglican Church, like everything else to do with England, was in decay, tired, worn out, having lost its sense of mission, and I wished to make the most of it before it passed away altogether.

The commotion was centred on a woman propped up against the wall of the church and sitting on a flattened cardboard box; she was remonstrating with a policeman, and (whom I guessed to be) a young curate of the church was doing the very same. Passers-by had stopped to see what the fuss was all about. Voyeurism can always be relied upon to bring the crowds in.

"I ain't doin' no 'arm!" the lady was shouting.

"Come on now, madam, move on," the policeman was saying, as if the woman had some place to go.

"I would ask you kindly to desist," the young curate was telling the policeman.

It was then that I recognised the voice of the woman, though not the diction, which was not so refined as I remembered it. Then I recognised the face. But if that woman was *her* then who was the woman that I'd seen not five minutes before? What had happened to the manifold allurements of the woman of a few moments before, or even to those of the woman of fifteen *years* before?

Amid the polite verbal scuffling (the English could still put on a dignified commotion, it seemed), the woman's eyes peered up at me and told me that the recognition was entirely mutual. Her eyes implored me: "I don't want your money, still less your pity, only remember me for the person I was, not the person I became. Do *that* in memory of me."

That evening, at seven o'clock, I was due to celebrate my first Mass since my ordination five days before. I was not nervous about that. But I was nervous about what I was seeing now. Should I speak to her? If I do speak to her, what should I say? Should I do more than speak to her? Should I take her somewhere safe, as she had once led me—albeit unwittingly—to somewhere safer than safe? These were the questions that presented themselves to me as I stood there wondering what to do.

The prospect of celebrating my first Mass was a challenge, my lack of nerves notwithstanding. The situation in which I found myself, outside Saint Martin-in-the-Fields, was more challenging still, and I was nervous about it, more nervous than I had been at any time before or since that kiss.

Fragments

ONE

The elegantly attired young man (he was thirty-seven, which *is* young for most people alive today) strolled into the bistro and parked himself beside a barstool; he studied it for a moment as he wondered if he should attempt to mount it and then perform what was bound to be a delicate balancing act on the seat of the apparatus. He decided against it; instead, he awaited the appearance of the owner of the bistro, shuffling coins noisily in his hands and gazing at some indeterminate point amongst the hanging optics.

When the woman eventually appeared, she startled him.

"Good morning, Robbie!" The greeting was enthusiastic, for Robbie was not only one of her best friends, he was also her first customer after the breakfast rush.

"Hello, Jenny!" Robbie returned in kind, pleased as ever to see her. To himself, in a confessional moment of weakness, he admitted that he had designs on the woman, who was his age, highly attractive, and single. Indeed, she had always been single, or at least unmarried, as had he, and he continued to nurture the suspicion that the two of them were somehow meant for each other and only needed the most propitious circumstances for them to be brought together. The confessional moment slipped into a moment of self-censure, and he chided himself for coveting a woman who could never have been anything other than a friend.

"What can I get you?"

"I'll have a cappuccino, please."

"I've some croissants left over from breakfast. Would you like one? They need eating."

"How could I possibly refuse?"

"Take a seat at a table. I'll bring them over."

"Will you join me?"

"I will, yes."

TWO

"Louise will be here in an hour or so."

At these words of Jennifer's, Robbie Grayling shuffled uneasily in his chair and drank, guiltily, frothy coffee from his mug. He stared vacantly out of the window and beheld pensioners dragging shopping trolleys behind them as if they contained lifetimes of personal baggage, heavy, and laden with regret, sadness at missed opportunities, and despair at the lack of time left to embellish the past with hope for the future. Then he saw children and knew that they would be just like the pensioners seven decades hence. The parents were somewhere between the children and the pensioners: for them, it was neither too early nor too late, but he saw even in them too much of the cares of this world, so much so that he wondered why people chose to burden themselves with responsibility for others, as if responsibility for themselves were not burden enough to carry through life. He had chosen a bachelor's life and childlessness for himself, and about that he had few if any regrets.

"And?"

"She's really struggling, Robbie." Jenny dared to say so, knowing that her words would provoke profound unease in her friend.

"Yes, I know but..." He returned his gaze to the window, this time seeing through and past all before him, his feelings dimmed as he searched for the right words. "There's a limit to what I can do for her, Jenny, you must see that. I'm her late husband's brother. That's all. We barely know each other."

"What do you mean? You've known her all your life."

"I know...but, well, she's always been a mystery to me."

"What about Elsa?"

"Elsa's my niece. That's all. If I start overdoing the charity, they'll become dependent on me."

"They're dependent on *me*."

Robbie sighed. He was all too aware that his brother had left Louise and Elsa with nothing, and that Jenny had been shouldering a burden that should have been as much his as it was hers.

"And I'm just her *friend*," Jenny added, she, too, mindful that even what she continued to sacrifice for Louise Taylor and her daughter Elsa was nowhere near enough to keep the wolf from the door.

"I do what I can for Louise," Robbie said. "I know she's struggling. Sebastian drank himself to death and left her penniless. I go round to her place a couple of times a month. I take her shopping. I buy her food."

"I know."

"She's not in a good place."

"She comes here most days, at around midday, and I feed her and the girl with leftovers, but their being here is bad for business, what with Louise moping around and Elsa running around disturbing all my customers. It's so annoying. I nearly exploded yesterday."

"I'm not sure what we can do about it."

"She'll be here shortly. Why don't you stay and chat with her?"

"What can I say to her that I haven't said already?"

"Just being here with her—being here *for* her—would make a difference, I'm sure."

"I'm going to her flat tomorrow morning. It's Elsa's fourth birthday. I've a present for her."

"Oh, thanks for reminding me. I need to buy her something."

"It's the girl I'm more worried about," Robbie said. "She hasn't had the best of starts in life."

"You and I are pretty much all Louise and Elsa have," Jenny told her friend sadly. "We have to do something for them."

"We *are* doing something."

"But is it enough?"

Life outside the bistro went on in its usual aimless way, as people came and went, shuffling up and down the street like chess pieces being moved by players lacking either strategy or conviction. A young mother struggled to contain the transgressive exuberance of her three offspring running and leaping and bounding around her, and her task was not made easier by the infant screaming inside the pushchair, which conveyance stubbornly refused to submit to her will, when all she wanted it to do was move forward with her in a straight line. An old man with a pronounced stoop shambled by like a snail in hot pursuit of a tortoise.

"Was there ever anything between you and Louise, Robbie?"

Stunned, Robbie thought about the question. He was bound to wonder if Jenny really had just put those words to him, and in so sudden and abrupt a fashion.

"No!" he replied. "Why do you ask?"

"There *were* rumours, Robbie."

"In this provincial backwater, as well you know, people have nothing better to do than gossip."

"I know, but it's just that, well, I've often sensed an atmosphere between you two ... you know, tension ..."

"What kind of tension?"

"As if there's unfinished business between you two ..."

"You're barking up the wrong tree, Jenny."

"Forget I mentioned it. I'm sorry."

Jenny became distracted by the man who had entered the bistro and who was now standing at the bar waiting to be served. He wore a long black wool-and-cashmere coat, and a red scarf was wrapped around his neck in the style of a student at college. He was tall and had a full head of dark hair. He was aged somewhere between thirty and forty, but closer to thirty, surely. He was handsome but strangely unmanly with it; a person of almost indeterminate sex; a visitation from a world of androgynous creatures searching for a safe place in a strange, indifferent land.

"Do you know him?" Robbie asked Jenny, having noticed her fixation with the newcomer.

"He's been coming here for a few weeks now, on and off," Jenny said. "He drifts in, and he drifts out. He stands at the bar, brooding, not saying a word. He has a couple of drinks. Then he pays and leaves."

"So, he's a quiet chap," Robbie said. "What's wrong with that?"

"There's *nothing* wrong with it. I like that about him. It makes a change from guys coming in here and hitting on me."

"Has he ever tried talking to you?"

"Never ..."

"Have you ever tried talking to him?"

"Once or twice, you know, small talk ..."

"Any joy?"

"The occasional sigh, the odd word, but nothing conversational ..."

"You seem to find him interesting." Robbie was trying to conceal his jealousy, for he knew that Jenny had a weakness for men of mystery.

"I'm just curious, that's all. I'd like to know his story."

"How do you know he *has* a story?"

"*Everyone* has a story. Most people's stories are boring. But his? Well, I sense something quite intriguing about him."

"Why don't you ask him?"

"Why don't *you* ask him?"

"Me? Why me?"

"Because I can't get a word out of him. Perhaps he will respond to you."

"But I don't want to know his story, even if he has one to tell, and I dare say he doesn't want to share it with me."

"Don't give me that," Jenny said with a cheeky smile. "I can tell you're curious."

"You're wrong."

"Come to the bar with me. Chat to him while I serve him."

"Do I have to?"

"You're always telling me how good you are with people, how naturally you connect with strangers, so now's your chance to prove it to me."

"All right, but, if he makes it clear that he wants to be left alone, I walk away, okay?"

"It's a deal."

THREE

The stranger stood at the bar with a beer in his hand. Jenny had poured Robbie a beer, on the house, and he stood leaning with his right elbow on the bar searching his prospective companion's features for signs that he was prepared to engage, man to man. He felt like a cat waiting to pounce on a mouse as soon as the prey dared to move.

Eventually, much to Robbie's surprise, the stranger spoke.

"Are you a photographer?"

"I might be."

"I just wondered why you're standing there, sizing me up. Either you're a photographer or you're trying to pick me up."

"I could be both," Robbie said. "But I'm neither."

"I'm glad to hear it."

"My name's Robbie. I try not to use my full name: Robert Daniel Grayling. I don't use the letters before and after my name either. I don't like to seem pompous, you see."

The stranger's eyes darted upwards at Robbie, as if to acknowledge that there might be potential for fellowship between them.

"My name's Edward Morgan," he replied. "Family calls me Eddie. Friends call me Morgan."

"Well, since I'm not family, but I might yet be a friend, I shall call you Morgan."

"As you wish…"

"Cheers, Morgan…" Robbie raised his glass.

Morgan raised his glass in turn. "Cheers," he said.

Robbie glanced at Jenny, who was serving a customer; she shot Robbie with a look of approval, for his start with the newcomer was promising.

"Are you new in town?" Robbie asked.

"I've been here about a month."

"The only reason why anyone comes to this most deadbeat of deadbeat towns is because it's dirt cheap."

"I'm a freelance graphic designer, so I can live pretty much anywhere."

"And, of all the towns in the world, you chose *this* one?"

"Like you said, it's cheap, and mortgages are hard to come by."

"Stick around and things might pick up." Robbie chuckled to himself. "You never know, one day this town might be fashionable."

"Here's to it." Morgan raised his glass again.

Robbie followed suit. Then he asked Morgan where he had come from to seek dubious refuge in their unassuming little town.

"If it's all the same to you, I'd rather not say."

"Oh, I see," Robbie said respectfully. "You wish to remain a mystery."

"Perhaps," Morgan replied. "But not to you, nor to anyone else, but to *myself*."

Robbie pondered Morgan's words and wondered if he had not got himself into a situation that was way over his head. He felt totally out of his depth with the mysterious stranger. He dared himself to ask another question and be confounded yet again. He dared not ask. Instead, he decided to tell Morgan something about himself, anything, in the hope that Morgan would reciprocate with information of his own.

"I've lived in this town all my life. I was born here. My first memory is of the sun setting behind the old glue factory. I went fishing in the river here once, as a child, and all I caught was a supermarket trolley loaded with Tesco bags filled with dead rats. My childhood sweetheart was called Lisa. When I got a job in the said glue factory, she questioned my ambition and dumped me. I wouldn't have minded, but it was only a summer job whilst I was at school. I *did* have my sights set on bigger and better things. Then we got back together. Then, when I left school, I got myself a proper job, as a trainee accountant, at the cement works next to the glue factory. She dumped me again, saying that I was destined to remain a prisoner in this deadbeat town for the rest of my days. I'm thirty-seven now and Lisa remains the closest I've ever come to unmitigated happiness."

"Where is Lisa now?"

"She works on the checkout at the Tesco down by the bus station."

"You've never married then?"

Robbie shook his head sadly. "I'm unmarried and childless, and I guess I always will be."

"What's your line of work now?"

"I'm still an accountant. Chartered. I have my own practice, in the High Street. This is my coffee break. Or should I say *beer* break?"

"There's a woman who comes in here. Her name's Louise. She comes in here every day with a little girl. She's nice. They're *both* nice."

"Do you talk to Louise?"

"The odd word..."

"Would you like me to introduce you to Louise? She's my sister-in-law."

For a moment, Morgan pondered Robbie's revelation. He shook his head. "I observe people," he said. "I don't engage with them if I can help it."

"Very wise," Robbie said. "Keep your distance. People are dangerous. They're like snakes. They bite." He smiled at Morgan to show that his joke had some basis in truth. "Does Louise ever talk to you?"

"Not really. She arrives, lends Jenny a hand, drinks coffee, eats something, chats with Jenny, but she leaves me be. Sometimes, she looks at me, as if she's trying to work out if I'm not some kind of apparition. She might say the odd word to me."

"And the girl?"

"She runs around the place, pestering the customers, in the nicest possible way, of course."

"This might seem a strange question, but..."

"Yes?"

"Does Louise seem happy to you?"

"She seems sad. True, she busies herself about the place, and she's full of energy and life, but I can tell that she's troubled."

"Aren't we all?"

"Why do you ask?"

"I just thought that you, as an outsider—well, a new-comer—might have a different perspective, that's all."

"Okay . . ."

"Louise was married to my brother, Sebastian. He died about a year ago. He was a drinker and the drink killed him. He had no excuse to drink. He had a perfectly idyllic child-hood. Louise is not the easiest of women to live with, but it wasn't she who drove him to drink."

"What—or who—was it then?"

"He never told me. He never told anyone. My own brother became an alcoholic and I have no idea how or why. So much for brotherly love."

"Perhaps this town drove him to drink?"

"That's entirely possible."

"My impression is that a lot of people in this town drink too much."

"Yes, and the most sober people I know in this town work for the brewery."

Morgan gave a little laugh. He looked at his watch. "Louise will be here any minute now."

Robbie nodded. "As soon as she walks in, I shall leave. I shall make it look like I was leaving, anyway, of course. As you can see, my beer is almost drunk."

"Like that between you two, is it?"

"It is," Robbie replied, "but we have our moments."

Right on cue, the door opened and in stepped Louise with the girl scampering in her wake. Robbie had his back to the door, but he knew who had just entered the bistro behind him. It was time for him to make a discreet exit. He turned round to face the incomers.

"Hello, Louise," he said. "I was just leaving."

"Of course, you were," Louise replied cynically.

"I have work to do."

"See you tomorrow then."

"I'll bring little Elsa's present round, yes." At the door, he looked over his shoulder and told Morgan that he would see him soon.

Morgan raised his nearly empty glass in acknowledgement and nodded his approval. He was looking forward to seeing his new friend again. He sensed fellowship between them, a mutual attraction even, which was founded on nothing more illicit than tenderness.

The feeling was entirely mutual.

FOUR

As luck—or fate—would have it, the two men met again that very evening, in the Angel and Greyhound pub, in the town centre. It was the type of pub that could be as busy on a Tuesday night as on a Saturday night. Neither was the type of man to hide away in the snug, so neither was surprised to see the other propping up the bar in the saloon.

"We have to stop meeting like this," Robbie said, deploying an icebreaker that has stood the test of time.

"I guess we just hang out in the same exciting places," Morgan joked in reply.

"So, should I expect to run into you in the Kitten Club?"

"I doubt that very much."

"Can I get you another?"

"Sure!" Morgan said. "Thanks!"

Neither man spoke until their glasses had been replenished. It was as if their conversation required alcohol to fuel it. Silence, however, bothered neither man, for each was reflective and possessed the gift of contemplation. As the drinks were poured, then, the two men looked around and immersed themselves in the hum of chatter and the putative awakening of people's spirits occasioned by the liberal consumption of alcohol.

Morgan mentioned that there had been an incident in the bistro, involving Louise, just after Robbie left.

"Really?" Robbie said. "What kind of incident?"

"Louise was talking to Jenny, distracting her from her work. You know how she talks. Urgently, as if every little detail of her life were a major drama."

Robbie nodded sagely. "I know all too well," he said.

"And, as she was chatting away, the girl, Elsa, was running around the place annoying all the customers. Then the girl knocked someone's glass of beer off his table and, well, Jenny exploded."

"I can't say I'm surprised to hear that," Robbie said. "That girl has been an accident waiting to happen for too long."

"Jenny hit the roof. Some of what she said to Louise was deeply personal. Quite unpleasant, if truth be told."

"What exactly did Jenny say?"

"She said that Louise had been sponging on Jenny for too long, and that she should find herself a meal-ticket somewhere else."

"It had to be said."

"Maybe so, but Louise had a go back, grabbed the girl by the hand, and stormed out of the bistro. The customers were not impressed."

"I bet they weren't."

"What kind of relationship do Jenny and Louise have?"

"They go way back," Robbie said, his voice touched by nostalgia. "We all do: myself, Jenny, Louise, and, of course, Sebastian. We all grew up together; we went to the same schools; and we stayed in this town."

"Has Jenny never married?"

"No man could ever meet her impossibly high standards."

"Is she with anyone now?"

"Not as far as I know." Robbie saw that Morgan was lost in thought and he surmised that Jenny was very much on his mind. "I've been friends with her for too long even to consider going out with her. Though I have had the occasional fantasy about hooking up with her. But you? Well, you're free to ask her out. Louise too. She's single. Though she comes with more baggage than Heathrow Airport."

"What about *you* and Louise?"

"What about us?"

"Anything between you two?"

"I won't lie to you. There was something between us a while back."

"When your brother was married to her?"

"Well, yes, sort of," Robbie said. "Let's not go there."

The two men paused for refreshment; they drank their beer in synchrony, as if directed by a choreographer somewhere in the background; and the way they moved seemed (even to them) to be in keeping with what they were thinking and feeling at that moment in time.

"So," Robbie resumed, his tone jocular, as if he were about to goad Morgan with light-hearted banter, "which one are you interested in?"

There was no reply from Morgan, only a vacant stare into the distance.

Robbie prompted his friend. "Jenny or Louise?"

"Oh, neither." Morgan's words were broken a little, and they stumbled out in three or four fragments of melancholy and regret: the latter because, under different circumstances, he would have found either woman, in her own way, deeply enticing.

"Look," Robbie said gently, "it's none of my business what—"

"I'm not gay, Robbie, if that's what you're suggesting."

"No, no, I . . ."

"I'm what life has made me," Morgan said. "I can't change now, much as I'd like to."

"I could say much the same, my friend."

"I don't want to sound mawkish, and I don't want you to think that I'm permanently and irretrievably damaged by what's happened in my life, but I'm finding it impossible to shake off the past. It's like it's stuck to me."

"I understand that completely, Morgan. Whatever's happened to you, you're entitled to deal with it in your own way."

"People the world over have experienced worse—much worse—than I have, and they've dealt with those experiences better—much better—than I have, but we all deal with trauma in different ways. We're none of us machines."

"Quite right!"

"My mother left me when I was eight years old. I was an only child. My father turned to drink. I never saw my mother again. I've no idea why she abandoned me and my father and never came back, or why she never got back in touch. It was like she went up in a puff of smoke. When I was twenty, I met a woman, the perfect woman. We cared deeply for each other. We'd both had difficult childhoods. We gave each other strength. We were each other's rock. Our relationship never once hit the rocks. We married. Our marriage was perfect. Yet, two years into our marriage, my wife left me. She's never uttered a word by way of explanation. I'm completely in the dark."

"I'm so sorry to hear that."

"I'm at a loss to explain either … whatever you want to call it … abandonment …"

"Like you said just now, people aren't machines," Robbie said. "They do things that even they themselves can't explain."

"At least Jordan—my ex-wife—had the decency to stay in touch. Well, she had to, I suppose, to make arrangements for the divorce. Since the divorce, I've not heard a word from her."

"Has she married again?"

"No, but she's with someone. They have two children together. The man's … Well, I've never met him, so I can't say what he's like."

"Keep out of their way. That's my advice, for what it's worth. Maintain a dignified silence."

"I've no wish to know what goes on between the two of them."

"She's long gone. Someone else will come along."

Morgan shook his head. "I'm better off on my own."

"That makes two of us."

The two men smiled in solidarity with each other. They were forging an understanding quicker than either had expected.

"I don't know what kind of person I'd be if my mother and my wife had behaved differently," Morgan said. "Much the same, I dare say," he laughed. "Morose and lugubrious."

"You don't have to apologise to anyone for being the person you are, Morgan, least of all to yourself. I can sense some brokenness in you, but that brokenness is part of you, it is who you are. Don't let anyone try to change you."

"I doubt that anyone *could* change me."

"Same again?" Robbie said.

"It's my shout," Morgan replied.

"It is, but this round's on me."

"If you're sure…"

"We can drink to bachelorhood."

"I'm all for that."

FIVE

Detective Inspector Sean Meredith was an angular man with sharp features, not the least of which was a nose long and pointed enough to harpoon a fish swimming in shallow water.

Deep water is what everyone present was in as they struggled to come to terms with what had happened overnight. Nobody gathered around the bar of the bistro was speaking. The little girl had been crying and Jenny had consoled her; now, little Elsa was silent, all tears spent and her feelings numbed by a compound of excruciating pain and bewilderment. Robbie and Morgan exchanged knowing glances. Then Robbie studied the policeman and wondered if Sherlock Holmes had not stepped out of the pages of Sir Arthur Conan Doyle and into Jenny's Bistro and the crisis that had engulfed it. The clothes were different, but the physique and countenance could not have been less unlike those of the great fictional detective. Meredith's young sidekick, Detective Sergeant Russell Wilson, stood by, visibly overawed by events, and Robbie waited for Meredith to say "Elementary, my dear Wilson", but, instead, the senior officer quizzed Jenny about events of the previous day.

"Look," Jenny stated, emphatically, "I admit that I lost my temper with Louise, yesterday, but I can't believe that that's the reason why she's disappeared."

"What exactly did you say to her?" the patient Meredith asked.

Jenny looked guilty, ashamed even. "I was rather harsh," she said.

"How harsh exactly?"

"Elsa was running around the restaurant like a headless chicken, and Louise was going on and on about something in that scattergun way of hers, and I was trying to serve customers, and, when the girl knocked the man's beer onto the floor, I just, well, you know, erupted."

"What did you say to her?" Meredith was forensic in his probing.

"I told her that she and Elsa should find somewhere else to hang out every day, and that she should stop sponging on me."

"Sponging?"

"I usually gave them lunch: leftovers, you know. Louise is struggling on benefits, I appreciate that, but I can't be their meal-ticket forever, can I?"

"And how did Louise react to your … eruption?"

"First, she was stunned. She looked at me in disbelief. Then she gave me an earful, grabbed Elsa by the hand, and stormed out."

"What exactly did she say?" Meredith was threatening to slice through Jenny with his relentless, razor-sharp questions.

"Something like: 'The truth is coming out now. You've never really liked me, have you? I know when I'm not wanted. Don't worry, Elsa and I won't darken your door again. We'll go someplace where we're not considered a burden and a nuisance.' She was shouting."

"Where might this other place be?"

"God knows."

Meredith turned to Robbie, who braced himself for some unpleasant questions.

"Mister Grayling," he began. "You reported Louise's disappearance, I understand."

"I did," Robbie answered.

"Tell me exactly what happened, please."

Robbie took a deep breath as he prepared to recount what had been for him a harrowing sequence of events, and not just for him.

"I went to Louise's flat at ten, as agreed. Today is Elsa's fourth birthday. I had a present for her. Elsa answered the door. She had to stand on a chair to do so, the poor girl. 'Mummy's not here,' she said. I went inside, spoke with Elsa, and established that Louise must have left sometime during the night, or early this morning."

"Did she leave a note?"

"No …"

"Has she ever done something like this before?"

"Not to my knowledge …"

Meredith looked at Jenny for confirmation.

Jenny shook her head.

"Knowing Louise as you do, Mister Grayling, what was her state of mind, do you think?"

"After the altercation with Jenny, and on top of everything else that's been going on in her life since Sebastian died, distressed, I would say, though I attach no blame whatsoever to Jenny for that."

"Thank you, Robbie!"

"I'm not being sarcastic."

"Oh, I know you're not," Jenny replied sarcastically.

"Has either of you any idea where Louise might have gone, any idea at all?" Meredith asked.

"I've told you, no," Jenny pleaded.

"Could she have left town?"

Jenny shrugged her shoulders. "This town's all she knows," she said. "I doubt that she's gone too far afield."

Robbie nodded his agreement. "That's how it is with Louise," he said. "Wherever she's gone, it's somewhere in this town."

Four faces turned to Morgan, as if *he* might have been able to shed light on the matter, an idea that amused the new man in town as much as it surprised him.

"Don't look at me," he said, blushing like a schoolboy caught raiding the tuckshop. "I'm new here. I wouldn't have a clue."

Meredith looked pensive for a moment. "Would it be fair to say that Louise would have to be in a pretty distressed state of mind—unbalanced, one might say—to disappear and leave her four-year-old daughter at home, alone?"

"I think that goes without saying, Inspector!" Jenny snapped back, not enamoured with the question.

"On Elsa's birthday too," Robbie added.

"As you know, we cannot consider a person missing until they've been absent for forty-eight hours," the policeman said. "However, under the circumstances"—he nodded at the crestfallen Elsa—"we'll put a few uniformed officers on the lookout."

"Thank you," Jenny said. "I'll make some coffee," she added. "It's on the house."

As the hostess busied herself with the coffee, the other four grownups present regarded each other with glum faces, each one imploring the others to offer suggestions as to where—anywhere, no matter how unlikely—Louise might have gone.

Robbie picked Elsa up and placed her on a barstool. The girl was so unresponsive that she might have been a doll.

"Yesterday morning," Morgan said, his words a welcome irruption in the oppressive silence, "I spoke with Louise for the first time."

"What did you speak about?" Meredith asked.

"It was only small talk," Morgan replied. "We exchanged a couple of sentences, that's all."

"What exactly did you say to each other?" Meredith pressed.

"I said hello, introduced myself, and asked her how she was. She told me that she was having the kind of day that made her want to jump off the top of the Devil's Finger."

Nobody present wanted to hear that. It was the last thing they wanted to hear. It was the last thing they *expected* to hear. The mood in the room dropped further, to a level commensurate with a fall from the very rocky outcrop just invoked by the unsuspecting newcomer to the town: unsuspecting, since he could not have known the significance of what Louise had told him.

"What is the Devil's Finger?" Morgan enquired, picking up on the general sense of unease.

Jenny enlightened him. "It's a notorious spot, out on the cliffs by Headley Bay," she said. "People often joke about jumping from the top of the Devil's Finger when they're having a bad day," she went on.

"Let's hope that Louise *was* joking," Meredith put in.

Coffee was taken in silence.

SIX

Whatever the tide had been when Louise jumped, it was almost at its height when her body was retrieved and lifted by a helicopter winch to the top of the cliff and then whisked away. In the wind and rain, people stood atop the cliff grappling with both the elements and their emotions. Elsa was in hospital, being treated for shock. Wilson had taken her there.

"It's all my fault," Jenny cried into Robbie's chest.

Usually, Robbie hated it when women poured tears onto his clothing, but he was wet, anyway, because of the rain, so he could hardly object on this occasion.

"You can't blame yourself," Robbie said. "You couldn't have known this would happen."

"I don't need platitudes now, Robbie."

Morgan felt as if he were intruding on private grief, as if he knew those with him nowhere near well enough to be sharing that moment with them, that heart-rending, soul-sapping moment from which they would struggle to move on. He wanted to say something soothing, but his tongue was tied into a thousand knots. He looked away from the entwined Robbie and Jenny and out to sea. Seagulls were diving and soaring and filling the air with their mocking cries, whilst waves crashed into the rocks below, one thunderous blow after another. Vast black plains of water rolled towards the shore from their source in the far distance, as if they were being discharged with a vengeance by a distempered horizon.

"I'll be on my way then," Meredith announced. "This is not a police matter, it would seem, but, should you need to contact me, you know where to find me."

Jenny pulled herself away from Robbie and nodded her gratitude at the policeman.

"Thank you, Inspector," Robbie said.

With Meredith gone, something came over Jenny which she could not explain at the time and has not been able to explain since, for she turned on her friend quite suddenly and not without a savage turn of phrase.

"You have to take some responsibility for this, Robbie!"

Robbie was aghast. "What? Why?"

"Come on, Robbie! You know why! Louise told me a hundred times that Elsa is your child! She told me that Elsa couldn't possibly have been Sebastian's child, because he was in rehab at the time of her conception! Louise had to deal with Sebastian's drinking, with her infidelity with you, with the knowledge that Elsa was yours, and then with Sebastian's death! After Sebastian died, all she wanted from you was an admission that you were Elsa's father! But you denied it! You sidestepped your responsibility!"

"Not here, Jenny, and not now . . ."

"Right now, and right here, Robbie!"

"I invited Louise to prove that I'm Elsa's father. I made myself available for a DNA test."

"Oh, how very noble of you! She didn't want science! She wanted romance! If you cared enough about her to take advantage of her whilst her husband was away, you should have cared for her when her husband—your own brother—was dead!"

"It wasn't like that."

"The unresolved issue between you and Louise had festered for too long, Robbie! It took its toll on her!"

"Can we talk about this another time?"

Morgan wished to make himself scarce, but he did not fancy slipping away like a coward; neither was he keen to take a shortcut to the beach. So, he stood rooted to the spot, half-hoping that the ground would swallow him up.

"You! Me! Both of us, Robbie! We killed Louise! We have blood on our hands!"

"When did you become so melodramatic, Jenny?"

Jenny disappeared into the mist and swirling rain, up over the spur of the cliff and down the other side, towards the car-park on the outskirts of town.

For a second, Robbie's mind jolted him with formalities: the funeral to arrange, care for Elsa, finances, and sundry other legal matters; but he cast such thoughts out of his head and out to sea, to a place where even the ravenous seagulls could not find them.

The scenario might have seemed strange, even a tad comical: two men close to the edge of a cliff, standing facing each other, speechless both, as a storm brewed around them and seagulls worked themselves into a frenzy.

Eventually, one of them spoke.

"She's right, you know, Morgan."

"About the girl?"

"About everything…"

"What do you know about the Law of Unintended Consequences?"

"I know a lot about the Law of *Foreseeable* Consequences."

"Elsa will suffer for a time, but she'll get stronger."

"I know," Robbie conceded with sadness. He put his head in his hands. "Oh, God, I've messed up totally."

Morgan sighed. He chided himself for having been so tactless in his last remark, and he was overtaken suddenly by the urge to console his new friend. "You're a decent man, Robbie, whatever's happened here."

"Thanks, but I'm a cad and a bounder, and that's putting it mildly."

"Nobody's perfect, Robbie."

"I'll have to take Elsa into my care, of course," Robbie declared solemnly. Part of him was relieved that the matter, at long last, had been resolved, even if the circumstances could hardly have been worse.

Morgan offered Robbie a smile of sympathy, and part of *him* was wickedly pleased that he was not alone in having to endure drama after drama in affairs of the heart.

The two men took a step towards each other and embraced.

"Welcome to the family," Robbie said.

"Thanks for having me," the other replied.

They were still embracing, in a manner of speaking, as they followed in the footsteps of Meredith and Jenny and made their way home.

Getaway

Any one of the many seagulls soaring and swooping in the sky high above could have looked down on the sandy beach and seen the young man and the young woman racing each other to the water's edge. The man was in the lead, though it was apparent that he was holding back to allow the woman to catch him up and then to overtake him. She duly reached the water first and then took a few playful steps backwards to avoid getting her feet wet. He caught up with her and, standing behind her, put his arms around her waist, taking care not to squeeze her too tightly. She took his hands in hers and then tipped her head back as he kissed her neck. After a minute or so locked in such embrace, they both removed their shoes and began paddling in the water, she with her skirt hitched and he with his jeans rolled up around his knees. A few people strolled up and down and across the beach, some of them with dogs, but only the lovers had been brave enough to enter the water.

"Why's it so cold?" she wondered aloud.

"Because it's the North Sea…"

"No, I meant the weather. It's the middle of May, but it's so cold and windy. It's been a horrible week."

"Horrible?" he said, pretending to be hurt.

"The week's been fantastic, better than I ever imagined, except for the weather."

"And why's the week been so fantastic?"

"Well, you see, I met this guy and he's totally wonderful."

"It's funny you should say that, because I met this girl, who's amazing in every way, and she's made me the happiest man alive. I've been so dazzled by her beauty that I haven't even noticed the weather."

"She's so lucky, this girl of yours, to have met such a tender and romantic young man."

"*I'm* the lucky one."

The girl smiled beguilingly, not for the first time that week. "When we raced each other to the sea, did you let me win?"

"Yes, but you won much more than a race to the sea."

"What else did I win?"

"My heart…"

"And you mine…"

"This is a perfect moment. I've dreamed of such a moment."

They embraced again as waves lapped around their ankles and the retreating foam fizzed in dissipation. The seagulls were becoming restless, and more raucous, as if instinct told them that the tide had turned and that food therefore was bound to be more plentiful. The birds were indifferent to the human coming and going below, except insofar as it promised them food. They cared not for romance and the yearning for love that burdened every human heart on the beach beneath them. Theirs was a life where only the next meal mattered, and where survival was sought purely for the sake of survival.

The lips of the lovers touched so tenderly that they barely touched at all, caressing each other like two velvet cushions nestled together on a divan, and, sensing consummation, they withdrew. The embrace tightened, which was an act of supreme chastity amid the animus and carnality of nature in the raw. If the lovers' souls could have sung, even the birds would have put nature aside and joined them in mutual rapture, paying homage to their creator and the very begetter of love itself.

Though he wanted to say "I love you", he knew it was not the time. She, too, forbore, desisting for the sake of a propriety with which, at that moment, she felt not a scintilla of kinship. They wanted to release their feelings, to conform them to the melody, the sublime duet, of their souls; to let them take flight with the birds.

He peeled away from her, gentle as a husk floating in the breeze, and left her to commune with the sea. They had left their shoes on the beach, beyond the reach of the waves, and he stepped towards them. With his feet, he wrote two words, "Jason" and "Nina", before lying down on his back with his head just below the inscription of his name, with hers to his left.

"Dante once said that the only perfect view is the sky above one's head." He listened for the answer, but all he could hear were the cries of the birds and the breath of the waves as their whispering undulations broke and broke again on the shore. "But an Italian who had never been to England would say that, wouldn't he?" he added as he peered up at the slate-grey monochrome under the spell of which he was being held captive.

"Chaucer once said, 'Hard is the heart that loveth nought in May,'" she said by way of retort. "But I guess he didn't suffer from hay fever."

"Do *you* suffer from hay fever?" he asked, seeming to address the sky.

"Sometimes," was the reply, but not from the sky.

She tumbled theatrically onto the sand beside him and beheld that same overcast of grey into which, here and there, patches of a darker hue—shades of charcoal, no less—had insinuated themselves with suggestions of rain.

"What have you learnt about yourself during your time here?" Jason asked the question genuinely keen to know the answer, for there was so much about her that he wished to know, and he felt that the question would serve as the key that would open the box containing all her secrets. He reckoned that, if he got her talking about herself, she would open up and her natural reticence would be bypassed. He would catch her off guard.

She, however, was having none of that.

"I've learnt that I don't like cherry-flavoured ice-cream."

Jason was both moved and disappointed by the answer. He had been trying all week to garner information about Nina, but he had learnt nothing of any substance, and he felt cheated by her apparent determination to withhold even the most basic of details about her life and person. He wondered why she was so bent on remaining a mystery to him.

"I know virtually nothing about you," he ventured to say. Their heads were tilted towards each other now, earnestly, their eyes betraying the full force of mutual ardour. "You've told me so little about yourself."

"*I* don't know much about *you* either," she replied.

"I've told you much," he protested gently. "If I told you more, it would hardly be fair, given how little *you've* told *me*."

"I wish to preserve the purity of our…" She let the word drift, unspoken, into the salty air and be carried away by the breeze, forever to remain unsullied by speech, mere speech, that human act which has tarnished so many a noble sentiment.

"Say it," he urged her.

"You attach too much meaning to words," she said.

"Words are powerful."

"Silence, more so…"

He turned his face away from her and resumed his contemplation of the heavens; she did likewise, irked by his petulance, and awaited his next attempt to break her silence. Neither spoke for two or three minutes. They lay there, two people on a beach, forming the figure eleven, trying to tap into the thoughts and feelings of the other. A seagull landed behind them and fixed its beady eyes on them; it looked puzzled by the display of verbal constipation by two representatives of a supposedly superior species; it stabbed at the sand with its beak, trying to skewer a worm; and then it flew away to join its companions, who were putting on a display of their own; a concert, no less, of cries and whelps of hunger and satisfaction; theirs a need for food, mere sustenance, with no thought for the myriad consolations of love.

"What have you learnt about *your*self?"

For a few seconds, Jason allowed Nina's words to float away, aimlessly, to go where they would, to find for themselves a resting place where they might be forgotten, never to be heard again, and so never to be answered. He thought about remaining silent, but wilful reticence was not *his* style. Anyway, what had he to hide? He would not allow tetchiness and a simmering rancour to insinuate themselves into their friendship, their amour, or whatever it was that bound them, on their last evening together. What they shared was too precious to spoil; as Nina had intimated, it was something pure; a gift that, as ever, was in the gift of the recipient to throw back in the face of the giver. Eventually, he spoke.

"Like you, I came here to find peace. I was overwrought, tired, exhausted. Meeting you here has reassured me: that there are people in the same boat as me, seeking the same escape, and the same sanctuary."

"But what have you learnt about your*self?*"

"That I *do* like cherry-flavoured ice-cream ..."

He searched her for signs that she had appreciated his joke, and she smiled in return, grateful for the chance to acknowledge her unfairness to him in being so guarded and reluctant to reveal herself to him.

"I've learnt that I'm too self-absorbed," he went on. "It's funny, isn't it? I came here for solitude and to reflect on my life. How self-absorbed is that? And, in being so self-absorbed, I've realised that I need to be *less* wrapped up in myself; that I should focus on doing more for *others,* and less for *myself.*"

"I spend my entire life looking after my sick father," Nina said, "so I could be forgiven for coming to the *opposite* conclusion about *myself.*"

Inadvertently, perhaps, he thought, she had revealed a little about herself, but he was loath to take advantage. He wondered who might be looking after her sick father now. Somebody, obviously, he reflected. Arrangements would have been made. Since the question did not need to be asked, he left it unspoken.

"Are you going back to work on Monday?" she asked him.

"Yes," he replied, "the Fitzwilliam Museum would not survive another week without me."

"I have to leave my chalet at ten o'clock tomorrow morning," she said with sadness, though part of her was quite relieved that normal life, arduous though it could be, was on the verge of returning.

"Stay with me tomorrow night."

The words came out like a volley of bullets from a gun, and in them was a note of desperation, as if he were pleading with her from a position of profound weakness which bordered on the helpless.

"I have to get back to my father."

"I don't leave until Sunday morning. We could leave together."

"I'll think about it," she said, "on one condition."

He sat up like a man waking up from a bad dream, only there was nothing bad about *this* dream.

"Name it," he said eagerly.

"That you go and buy me an ice-cream …"

"Consider it done!"

"But not cherry-flavoured …"

"That goes without saying," he said with a winning smile.

She sat up herself and surveyed the vast expanse of water before her.

"I shall sit here and watch the tide going out," she said.

"I'll be back in five minutes," he declared, and he trotted away from her in the direction of the Mermaid Café, scene of most of the meals they had taken together that week. He was happy. He was excited at the prospect of spending a night—the first of many nights, he hoped—with the woman who had captured his heart, and who might yet capture his soul.

He looked over his shoulder and saw Nina silhouetted by distance and the gathering gloom, and for a moment he was happier than he had ever been before.

Five minutes later—a time so painfully short that, whenever he found himself reflecting upon it once the holiday was at an end, he struggled not to weep—Jason emerged from the café and leapt onto the beach with his heart racing like a greyhound out of the traps. He nearly dropped the two strawberry Cornettoes that he was clutching excitedly when he surveyed the beach and realised that Nina was nowhere to be seen. Though it made no difference whether he remained where he was standing, or returned to the water's edge whence he had come, he went back, anyway, only to find what he knew he would find: a beach devoid of Nina, the imprints of two human bodies in the sand, and an ocean cruelly indifferent to his demand for answers. There were not even any footprints to give him a clue as to Nina's whereabouts. Nina had simply vanished.

Knowing that doing so would be futile, Jason went to Nina's chalet, and there he found the front door open; his heart beating with nervous anticipation, he went inside and found a distinguished-looking woman of about fifty years of age stripping the bed and piling up the sheets on the floor. When she saw Jason, she was startled.

"Can I help you?" she said with a trace of fear in her voice.

"Are you the maid?"

The lady bridled at that. "Actually, I'm Sarah Harper, the *owner* of this holiday park."

"Oh, well, I'm sorry to be so rude. I was looking for Nina."

"Who?"

"The lady who's been staying here this week…"

"There's been a young lady staying here this week," the lady replied, "but her name wasn't Nina."

"What *was* her name?"

"I'm not sure that it's my place to tell you."

Resigned to his fate, Jason shook his head. "It doesn't matter," he said. "When did she leave?"

"She left first thing this morning, a day early, as it happens."

"That makes sense. *She* called for *me* this morning."

"Are you a friend of the young lady's?"

"I thought I was."

"I'm sure you'll catch up with her, one way or another."

Jason shook his head again. "I know nothing about her," he confessed. "Now, I realise, I don't even know her name."

"What about Twitterbook or Facechat?"

Not even the tragically comic misnaming of the two social-media platforms was enough to raise him from the deepest, darkest pit of despair in which he languished.

"Like I said, I know absolutely nothing about her."

"I'm sorry for your troubles."

Jason drew some consolation from what appeared to be genuine concern for his welfare: he was crestfallen, and the lady seemed to feel for him. The kindness of a stranger was going a long way. Alas, he was sad that the woman knew his erstwhile lover's name, where she lived, and how to contact her, but that she neither could not nor would not divulge a single detail to put him out of his misery. What was hardest for him to accept—what was almost impossible for him to come to terms with—was that the girl whose name he had thought was Nina had plotted at least a day before to leave him high and dry. He felt as if he been led to the top of a mountain, and that it would be a long time before he got even halfway back down.

On the day that he departed that beautiful place by the sea, that beachside idyll, Jason stood on the very spot where he and Nina had lain. The imprints of their bodies had been washed away by the tide. He looked out to sea and wondered if she might not be out there somewhere. It would be an explanation, after all. She had disappeared in a few minutes flat, when, had she gone left or right, or even had she made straight for the path at the top of the beach, he would surely have spotted her in retreat. For, whichever way one looked or went, the beach was vast.

It seemed bitterly ironic to him that the hour of his departure, on that Sunday morning, should witness the first blue sky of his stay there. The seagulls looked different somehow—more vivid—against the backdrop of the cloudless sky. A flock of seagulls flew overhead like Red Arrows in formation.

"Which one is *you*, Nina?" he wondered as the birds glided majestically towards some unknown hideout.

A few yards along the beach, something was being washed up by the waves, as if it were being spat out by the sea, rejected for not belonging there, an alien thing that was not *of* the sea so had no place *in* the sea. He bent down to pick it up. It was Nina's red headband. She had worn it every day she had been with him, and her dark hair had flown behind it and down her back like waters of ebony in freefall. He examined it, thoroughly, and he turned it this way and that, looking desperately for a clue, any kind of clue, as to who Nina was. He prayed that a nametag would reveal itself. It was bound to be a futile prayer, as all his prayers ever had been.

Something, though—Providence, perhaps, if he could stretch his imagination that far, and that close, to a putative deity—had allowed this thing of hers to be separated from Nina and to fall into his grateful hands.

It was not much, but it was something, and it was *hers*, and he would treasure it for the rest of his forty-six days.

Healing

ONE

Dr Anthony Woodcock was a man of ascetic temperament, and his austere-looking office was a faithful reflection of that abstinent disposition. The only thing on display in his consultancy room, apart from a few books about psychology, was a framed certificate on the wall demonstrating to clients his right to practise as a professional psychologist. One might even attach the label "spartan" to Dr Woodcock; and, accordingly, as he sat opposite the man in a matching armchair, Julian Dewhurst suspected that the man he was paying to delve into his psyche would have been equally at home submitting himself to military discipline as he was acting as exemplar of orderliness and self-regulation in civilian life.

Julian had worked out (by recourse to *Who's Who*, in the august pages of which Dr Woodcock had insinuated himself courtesy of a now-fading eminence) that his interlocutor was around fifty-five years of age, nearly a quarter of a century older than himself. He had to admit that the doctor looked a decade or so older than his years, though his slicked-back grey hair and impeccable grooming endowed him with a gravitas rarely seen in the demure Suffolk market town, Sudbury.

Julian imagined what he himself would look like twenty-five years hence, and saw a man going to seed, his hairline receding, his waistline expanding, and jowls starting to take up prominent positions on the sides of his face. He did not dare make the image in his mind's eye smile, in case he was made to recoil from the apparent effects of old age on his teeth. Before now, he had rarely thought about age, but his passing thirty had signalled a watershed in his life which had served to remind him that he was not immortal and that he never would be.

He decided that, at lunchtime, he would still go to his favourite café, as planned, but that he would eschew his usual sausages, eggs, and chips in favour of something very much healthier. He was being frank with himself when he conceded that his principal motive for patronising Hillside Café, on the town's Market Hill, was the beguiling smile that always greeted him there: that of the owner of the establishment, the charmingly sensual Francesca Halford. Today, he would impress her, not with his intellect and social standing, as was his custom, but with his newfound penchant for healthy food instead. The possibility that his resolve would have crumbled by the time he reached the café did not occur to him as he sat there, waiting for Dr Woodcock to speak.

"Well, Mr Dewhurst," the psychologist said at last, "it would seem that our first session was not so traumatic that it forestalled a second consultation on your part."

"On the contrary, Dr Woodcock, I enjoyed our first session immensely, and I'm looking forward to more of the same."

The doctor had a notebook cradled in his lap, and he wrote a few words in it that Julian could not make out from a distance of three yards or so. He wondered what Dr Woodcock could have written, given that no words of any substance had so far been spoken during the early stages of the session. Throughout the consultation, the psychologist would lean forward slightly to make spindly entries in his notebook. The notebook itself consisted of page after page of expensive-looking sheen bound in leather. It was no ordinary notebook. For a man of Dr Woodcock's abstemious bent, it was an unlikely extravagance.

"Let us recap then," Dr Woodcock resumed. "Our first meeting was purely introductory."

"Just to be clear," Julian interjected before Dr Woodcock could say another word, "I *will* be charged for last week's session?"

"Oh, yes!"

"Right…"

"Would you like some water?"

"Yes, I think I would. It's warm in this room, and I've worked up quite a thirst."

"Something stronger, perhaps?"

"Such as?"

"Tea? Coffee?"

"Water will do nicely, thanks."

"As you wish…"

Dr Woodcock poured his patron a glass of water from the jug that sat regally upon the wooden table separating the two men. He remarked that the water had been flavoured with lemon, and that he hoped that Julian would not mind. Julian replied that he appreciated the embellishment and thanked his host for the refreshment.

"You told me last week that you have no psychological issues whatsoever, and that you want me to explain why you are quite so untroubled."

"That's right."

"That's a somewhat unusual proposition for me, Mr Dewhurst, since I'm used to people asking me to sort their heads out, having once got inside them."

"What I'm hoping you can do, Doctor, is offer me an explanation why, given that my brother and I are only a year apart in age—I am the elder—and that we grew up in the same house and suffered the same troubled upbringing, his life went totally off the rails and mine...well, I've lived a rather charmed life overall."

"Since your brother is not here to speak for himself, Mr Dewhurst, I'm not able to offer you any help where *he's* concerned."

"I appreciate that, Doctor. I mention him—his name is Justin, by the way—simply by way of contrast. We grew up in the same place, with the same people, yet our lives unfolded in entirely different ways. You are a highly respected behavioural psychologist, if I may say so, so I'm hoping you can shed some light on this apparent anomaly."

"No two people are the same, Mr Dewhurst, not even brothers, not even *twin* brothers."

"I understand that, Doctor, but you behavioural psychologists believe that behaviour is the learned response of an organism to a stimulus. Have I got that right?"

Dr Woodcock pondered the question awhile, his features compressed in the effort of thinking, before nodding sagely and replying, "Broadly speaking, yes."

"So, therefore, Justin and I, broadly speaking, should be similar people?"

"I cannot fault your reasoning, Mr Dewhurst." Dr Woodcock took a sip from his glass of water with all the deliberation of a Rodin sculpture contemplating motion. "However, the human psyche, for us behaviourists, cannot be viewed in such deterministic terms. One's genetic inheritance cannot be ignored when either explaining or predicting behaviour."

"Very well, Doctor. I'm entirely at your disposal. Where would you like me to begin?"

"You could begin by recounting the events of your childhood, the experiences that you and your brother shared, and then we will discuss your response to those experiences and your brother's. The comparison will be fruitful, I'm sure."

"Very well, Doctor…"

Julian told his story in such unaffected and undramatic fashion that he might have been reading that day's football results to an assembly of monks in the throes of meditation.

He began with a summary of his parents' marriage, which was a brief tale of squabbling, arguments, multiple tit-for-tat infidelities and, yes, fighting, the latter a sad reflection upon his father, who had been fond of impressing upon his sons the intrinsic evil of a man's ever laying so much as a finger on a woman in anger.

After the inevitable parting of the ways, formalised by the divorce, Julian's mother remarried and got her life in order, in contrast with his father, who, in the wake of a string of ill-fated love affairs, settled on an amour with a raven-haired siren by the name of Elaine Brennan, formerly Duncan; for a while, indeed, he even settled *with* her, after she and her progeny moved into the erstwhile matrimonial home of Martin and Caroline Dewhurst; herself a recent divorcee, Elaine was nursing the scars given by a troubled marriage and an acrimonious breakup.

The affair between Martin and Elaine turned out to be yet more tumultuous, yet more fissiparous, and yet more volcanic than either had been involved in before (and that is some indictment), until the final cataclysm rent them, to leave, first, a nuclear wasteland and, shortly thereafter, a lingering, smouldering ruin.

How to explain the evolution of what had been seen by those involved as a welcome "fresh start" into such a squalid state of human affairs? Julian had put it down to the fusion of two incompatible families: that of one man and his two sons with a woman and her son and two daughters. That the man and the woman, the ostensible heads of this doomed aggregation, were reprobates both, that neither was any more stable than a Molotov cocktail on a bonfire, rendered the arrangement foolhardy, reckless even, from the outset.

Having stated for the record that, in his more charitable moments, Julian was prepared to view Elaine Brennan as a woman who simply buckled under the strain of looking after five children (though he qualified the statement by saying that many another woman has taken on the same number of children, and more, without descending into barbarism), he went on to describe the episodes which together made up the brief but turbulent liaison between his father and the most notorious of all his many lovers.

In the beginning, he said, the woman was seen by the two Dewhurst boys as a kind of saviour, or if not a saviour then an angel, what with her kindly smile and gentle voice that bespoke compassion not only for others but also for herself, for she, too, had endured hardship in life and in love and wished to start anew, with the slate wiped clean.

To welcome Elaine and her children to the Dewhurst home, Martin had painted the kitchen walls anew, in Elaine's favourite colour, sky blue; however, before the paint was dry, Elaine had settled into her new home and begun hastening the honeymoon period towards a sorry and somewhat pre-cipitous end.

Martin was an engineer; his specialist field was building and maintaining flight-simulators for military aircraft, and this job sent him on assignments at Royal Air Force bases in all parts of the country; indeed, it was these long periods away from home that had occasioned and facilitated his serial adultery and that of his wife.

History, then, had been bound to repeat itself; and it did so with a vengeance.

A week after the inauguration of the new domestic arrange-ment (Martin had welcomed the newcomers with bunting and a litany of cheesy songs about fresh starts and homecom-ings), the man of the house was embarked on a four-week assignment near Inverness, at RAF Lossiemouth, and so had begun Elaine's reign of terror.

She started as she meant to go on, and she went on in the same vein for three years.

What she did can be described succinctly, and that is exactly how Julian described it.

The beating of the Dewhurst boys (and of them only) came first, and they continued even after the more insidious torments were brought into play. They were administered on the slightest pretext, for the sort of misdemeanours ordinarily meriting nothing worse than a telling off, or they were apportioned for no reason at all. They were random. They were arbitrary. They were harsh and cruel.

At mealtimes, Elaine would feed her own children first, and then either feed Julian and Justin an hour or so later or not feed them at all, all too often sending them to bed on empty stomachs.

At bath times, she would bath her own children first, at length and making great play of the weekly event, and then condemn Julian and Justin to bathing themselves in cold, dirty water.

Without justification, she would make Julian and Justin, individually, go and stand in the corner of the kitchen, in the dark, whilst the others watched television from the comfort of the living-room.

One time, Elaine's younger daughter wet her bed, and, in the middle of the night, the woman made Justin and the girl, Melissa, swap beds, so that Justin had to spend the rest of the night in a bed soaked in urine that was not his own.

"There was more, much more, Doctor, but that is the gist of it, and bear in mind that this all went on, day after day, night after night, for three long years. The cumulative effect was…well, I've told you."

Dr Woodcock cogitated over Julian's monologue for so long that Julian wondered if the man had not fallen asleep with his eyes open. He appeared to be breathing, so Julian ruled out death. Eventually, he spoke.

"Are you saying that this Elaine woman behaved in this appalling manner only when your father was out of the house?"

"Yes, either when he was working away, or at home but working nights."

"How did she behave when your father was in the house?"

"As if butter wouldn't melt in her mouth ..."

"Why did you not tell your father what was going on?"

"Oh, we did. One day, Justin and I plucked up the courage to tell him."

"What did he say?"

"He didn't say a word. He simply grabbed us both by our necks and banged our heads together, quite literally. It's funny. When my brother and I used to fight or squabble, our mother used to threaten to bang our heads together. But she never actually *did* it, nor would she ever have done so."

"Why did you not tell someone in your family, or someone in authority, like a teacher, or even social services?"

"To be honest, we simply accepted it as normal. After all, domestic rancour was all we'd ever known."

"But there was help available."

"In our innocence, we knew nothing about that."

"You ended up in the hands of social services, anyway."

"Yes, and it was the best part of our childhood by far. Blessed relief, it was."

"I can imagine, though it's possibly the saddest thing anyone sitting in that chair has ever told me."

"I ought to tell you about one more incident."

"Incident?"

"Well, yes, because it happened just the one time. To me, anyway. I can't speak for my brother on this one."

"Go on."

"One morning, I was ill in bed. I must have been properly ill because Elaine hadn't forced me to go to school, as she had done whenever I'd been ill before. We were the only two people in the house. She came to my room, stood by my bed, eyed me seductively, took off her clothes, and got into bed with me. She then forced me on top of her."

"You had sex with her?"

"Briefly, ineluctably, there had been penetration, yes. It was the sexual equivalent of the Evacuation of Dunkirk."

"How old were you at the time?"

"I'd just turned thirteen."

"How did you feel about it?"

"To be honest, I didn't feel at all violated. I mean, before, she'd only ever been wicked to me, so it made a pleasant change for her to be nice to me."

"You call that being *nice* to you?"

"That's how I saw it at the time."

"Did you ever tell your father about this?"

"I valued my life, Doctor."

"Why, do you think, did your father put you and your brother through such a terrible ordeal?"

"More to the point, why did he put *himself* through it all? Given all that had gone before in his adult life, why did he think that tying himself to an unhinged woman and her maleficent offspring was such a good idea?"

Dr Woodcock sighed, as if to draw a line under one stage of the interview before moving on to the next. He was ponderous, cocooned in thought, but in no way was he perturbed by what Julian had just told him, for he had heard much worse in his time as a counsellor; he was exercised by Julian's story, however, because it was unique, the particular circumstances and events described archetypal and yet woven into the fabric of mankind's vast unspoken mythology.

Dr Woodcock then drank some water, and Julian watched as the Adam's apple of the drinker bobbed up and down his throat like a lifebuoy in choppy water. He then made some notes in his book.

Julian, too, drank from his glass of water, before sitting back and waiting for Dr Woodcock to invite him to compare and contrast his own, Julian's, response to the events described with his brother's.

When the expected question was duly put to him, Julian expounded thus: as a child, Justin had been a constant thorn in the side of authority, to the extent that, having beaten up his geography teacher, he had been sent to borstal, where—even there—he had made a nuisance of himself, culminating in his having to spend two weeks in solitary confinement after calling the governor a follicly-challenged vagina (or words to that effect) and then giving him a bloody nose; after leaving borstal, he had made a half-hearted attempt at living on the right side of the law, only to start keeping the sort of company that paved the way for his being detained for five years at Her Majesty's pleasure. The offence for which he had been sent to jail was armed robbery of a high-street bank, though at the trial he had pleaded in mitigation that his sawn-off shotgun, unlike those of his fellow gang members, had not been loaded. The judge, a man of the world who had heard such baloney and bluster all too often during his distinguished career, had dismissed the plea of mitigation like a chambermaid with a feather-duster swatting away a fly.

Julian went on to say that Justin, for all his numerous brushes with the law, was not an evil person, and not even a *bad* person; he had simply become restless and agitated because of a childhood blighted by instability and permeated by wickedness, as a malodorous gas permeates a building and seeps into its very fabric. Julian hastened to add that none of what happened to Justin during his childhood should be used to *excuse* his brother's subsequent behaviour, though it might fairly be offered as an *explanation* for it.

Dr Woodcock rubbed his chin thoughtfully, leaned forward in his chair, and then reclined again, as if the manoeuvre somehow dislodged a few brain cells and facilitated the act of cogitation.

"And yourself, Julian? Tell me about your life."

"There's not much to tell, really. I've lived a blameless life. I never even got detention at school. I was never given lines. No teacher ever raised their voice at me. I passed all my exams with flying colours. I went to university and law school. I became a lawyer. Nothing that happened in my childhood has ever affected me in the slightest, not to my knowledge, at any rate."

"What about your relationships with women?"

"Well, I've never married, not yet, but I wouldn't read too much into that. I've had a couple of relationships, meaningful ones, that fell by the wayside."

"And your brother?"

"Oh, he's had a string of ill-fated love affairs. He'll never settle on anyone. To tell you the truth, he's an out-and-out misogynist. I can't repeat some of what he says about women."

"Do you think that his attitude towards women was shaped by his childhood?"

"Yes, without a doubt, but he needs to deal with it, because it's not healthy, is it?"

"Has he ever been violent towards women?"

"Never!"

"So, he limits his violence to geography teachers and prison governors?"

"As if that's any kind of mitigation, yes," Julian said with a wry smile.

"Compared with how he was when he was sent to prison, what kind of person was he when he came out?"

"He went inside a thorn in the side of polite society, and he came out exactly the same."

"As a lawyer, I trust you're familiar with the threefold purpose of prison?"

"Punishment, rehabilitation and deterrence, you mean?"

"Yes…"

"Well, he was punished, but he's barely rehabilitated, and prison didn't deter him from committing crime before he went inside, and it hasn't deterred him since he came out."

"He's persisted with a life of crime?"

"From what I've heard, yes. I've a few contacts out in Spain who keep an eye on Justin for me. He's had one or two brushes with the Spanish police, though so far only for what we might call petty crime."

"Armed robbery to petty crime represents progress in anyone's book."

"Petty crime is entirely in keeping with his rather aimless life out there, and there remains the suspicion that it's only a matter of time before he gets in with the wrong crowd and gets back into *serious* crime. Spain, after all, *is* crawling with British men of dubious moral character."

Dr Woodcock sighed again, and drank some more water, performing the same ritual as before, thereby signalling another change of direction in his questioning.

"How did your father and Elaine come to break up?"

"Elaine got pregnant. The child could not have been my father's, since he'd had a vasectomy."

"How did you feel when your father and Elaine broke up?"

"Elated, euphoric, ecstatic … The day that woman walked out of our lives for good was the happiest day of our lives. I was fifteen. Justin was fourteen."

"How did your father react?"

"He tried to top himself. Justin and I got home from school one day and found him on the sofa out of his head on sleeping pills. He'd left a note on the floor beside him, addressed to Elaine, saying that he couldn't go on without her. That's when we were taken into care."

"Were you not fostered?"

"Briefly, yes, by Mr and Mrs Williams, who lived in a big house on Cornard Road, but they couldn't cope with Justin's mood swings, so back we went into care. The authorities were keen to keep Justin and me together."

"Where is your father now?"

"He's in Sydney, Australia, chasing women all over New South Wales and beyond, I dare say. He's not as young as he used to be, but he's used to a sex life that would have crippled Casanova, so I doubt that he's become a Buddhist monk."

"Do you keep in touch?"

"No …"

"Do you keep in touch with your mother?"

"No …"

"When did you last see Elaine?"

"On that blessed day when she left us …"

"Where is she living now?"

"I've no idea."

"And her children?"

"Again, no idea…"

"What would you say if you saw Elaine now?"

"I would tell her that I pitied her."

Dr Woodcock was pensive again as he reclined in his chair and allowed Julian's words to settle in his mind. His patient had not given him any information that he was not able to process with consummate ease, and yet he was troubled by what he had just heard. He had heard worse before, of course, but it was Julian's clinical recollection and articulation more than the words themselves that had engendered such profound unease. He compared Julian's reaction to the events described with Justin's and he could not help but conclude that the latter's response was the more normal, the more understandable, and the more conducive to dispassionate analysis. But was that not his, Dr Woodcock's, challenge: to help Julian understand why he stepped out of a train crash unscathed, while his brother emerged broken and beaten and bent on revenge on the driver, the train company, and even his innocent fellow passengers? He had an inkling of what he might tell Julian, but he was not sure that Julian would hear it as anything other than highly speculative, unscientific, and even a tad spurious.

"The best I can offer you, Mr Dewhurst, by way of explanation, is that you were born exceptionally resilient, which has enabled you to weather the multiple storms that battered you during your formative years; which is to say, in effect, that your experiences during your early years have not formed you at all, and that something else has formed you, something not so easy to pin down."

Julian offered only inscrutable features in return: it was his way of scratching his head and stroking his chin inquisitively.

"I think I understand you," he said, his modesty entirely genuine.

"There is also the possibility—and this does not exclude my first postulation—that your young self was unconsciously determined—motivated, certainly—to make a success of his life in spite of its unpromising beginnings."

Both of Dr Woodcock's theories had occurred to Julian many times before during his life, but he was not about to tell his analyst that; instead, sensing that the doctor had exhausted his diagnostic possibilities, he indulged him by thanking him and even by suggesting that the doctor had expounded his theories with characteristic and renowned clarity.

Once the concluding pleasantries were over, and the discussion concerning possibilities for future sessions wrapped up, Julian shared with Dr Woodcock the one experience that *had* upset him as a boy, and that still bothered him to that day.

"Because of my name, boys at school used to call me Ju Dew, pronounced 'Jew Jew', so it soon became common knowledge at my school, and it remained common knowledge even after I left school, that I was Jewish."

"*Are* you Jewish?"

"No!"

"I see."

"The fallacy that I was Jewish got stuck inside people's heads, and, no matter what I told them to the contrary, they continued to believe that I was Jewish."

"Well, my classmates used to sing at me: 'Tony Woodcock's got a lot of problems.'"

"Why?"

"Because of my name…"

"I see," the unseeing Julian replied.

"How would you sum up, in a few words, your life so far, Mr Dewhurst?"

"Well, I feel as though I should have grown up a different person. I feel as if I've been hounded by normality. Benignant eyes are watching over me."

"And whose are those benignant eyes?"

"I've no idea."

TWO

The doorbell clanged in its usual dramatic fashion as Julian pushed the sturdy oak door and entered the Hillside Café, which is situated halfway up Sudbury's Market Hill and which affords an unobstructed view of the statue of Thomas Gainsborough, the painter, the town's most famous son. Unobstructed, that is, on five days of the week, for the market obscures the view on Thursdays and Saturdays: that day being Saturday, there was a commotion behind him as market traders bellowed at potential customers to come and purchase the very best fruit and vegetables, at prices that could not be beaten. The accents of the market traders were more South Essex than West Suffolk; some of them, indeed, were more South London. The sound of the bell was as evocative as it was welcome; for Julian, it was the best sound in the world, for it heralded his favourite food served by his favourite person, the café's proprietor, the delectable Francesca Halford. The smells, too, were reminiscent of his many previous visits, the mahogany of the furniture proving as always to be as prevalently aromatic as the food being cooked in the kitchen and being savoured by diners in the restaurant. Most of the customers were familiar to Julian because of their regularity.

"Hello, Julian!"

"Hello, Donald!"

"Hi, Julian!"

"Hello, Rose!"

"Nice to see you, Julian!"

"Nice to see you, too, Chris!"

Once he had run the gauntlet of felicitations, he hovered by the counter, waiting like an abandoned dog for Francesca to appear. When she emerged, she looked (to Julian's admiring eyes) gloriously flustered, her blonde hair dishevelled, as if it had not been brushed for days, or as if some lucky man had rearranged every strand of it during the act of love. He tried to banish the latter thought from his mind, for it was too painful for him to imagine another man, even a faceless man, making love to Francesca, sharing her bed, and expending with her enough passion to satisfy any couple for a lifetime.

"Julian!"

"Don't look so surprised, Fran," Julian replied, trying to hide his burning desire for her. "I'm in here six lunchtimes a week."

"Sorry, I was just in the kitchen dealing with a little crisis."

"Can I help at all?"

"No, thanks, it was just a problem with the dishwasher. It's fixed now."

"Is your chef here?"

"Oh, yes. George never lets me down."

"What about your little helper?"

"Lizzie? She's due any moment. Here she is now!"

A surly-looking teenager strutted in, dressed more for parading up and down a catwalk than waiting on tables. Though Francesca greeted her cordially, the girl merely grunted in reply. Francesca seemed neither irked nor offended by the girl's brusque demeanour. She was, Julian could not help but conclude, markedly more tolerant of teenage rudeness than he himself was.

"The rush is over, Lizzie," Francesca told the girl. "We just need two steak-and-kidney pies, one with mashed potato and the other with chips, both with peas, for table two. The order should be ready to serve now."

"Okay," the girl said, the words coming out of her mouth as if she had allowed them to seep out rather than coming out through any effort of her own.

"There's a bit of washing-up to do too."

"Okay…"

The girl sauntered away as if she were savouring a slow walk to an inviting sea or a sun-drenched beach rather than embarking on an afternoon shift in a busy café. Julian watched her go, marvelling at such indolence, and he recalled that never would he have been so indulged as a teenager had he dared ever to display such shiftlessness. Francesca watched Julian watching the girl, knowing what Julian was thinking.

"She's actually pretty good," Francesca said. "Like George, she never lets me down, and she's popular with the customers. They consider her rather exotic."

"How old is she?"

"Sixteen…"

"Sweet sixteen," Julian sighed, wistfully, as if he had been that age back in the mists of time.

Francesca smiled her winning smile. "It wasn't so long ago for you," she said.

"Long enough ago for me to lament my lost youth…"

"We're the same age, but I wouldn't want to be sixteen again."

"Nor would I…"

"Your usual?"

"Yes, please!"

"Sit down in your usual place. I'll bring us over some coffee."

"Are you joining me?"

"There's something I want to show you."

"I'm intrigued!" Julian was more than intrigued, but, in the name of decency, he kept his counsel.

"Give me a couple of minutes."

As he waited for his curiosity to be sated, Julian gazed out of the window and observed as Sudbury's busiest day of the week unfolded; though he enjoyed watching the world go by, none of what he saw registered with him for more than a few seconds, not least because excitement could not have helped but get the better of him.

Francesca rejoined him carrying a tray bearing two cups of coffee and a copy of that week's *Suffolk Free Press*.

"Thank you, Fran," Julian said with a kindly smile.

"Can you believe that the statue of Gainsborough has been vandalised again?" Francesca said as she stared across the road at the partially obscured monument.

"Yes, I noticed," Julian replied. "Yellow paint's been tipped over it."

"The statue had only just been cleaned of the red paint that was tipped over it last week."

"The town's full of hooligans nowadays, I'm afraid."

"Every shopfront on the Market Hill has CCTV, yet the police cannot identify the culprits."

"It would help if the cameras were pointing in the right direction."

"Criminal damage, isn't it?"

"In law, yes, it is."

"On a more cheerful note, what are your plans for today?"

"I went to see a psychologist this morning."

"Oh?"

"Don't worry, it was just an academic exercise, really."

"Oh . . . "

"This afternoon, I'm going to watch Sudbury Town play Bury Town."

"But you don't like football."

"My company sponsors Sudbury Town's shirts. It's a big game, apparently, what they call a 'local derby'. There's no love lost between the two teams. I've been told to wear a flack jacket and a tin hat."

"Oh, very fetching!"

"This evening, I'm going to watch a film at the Quay Theatre."

"Oh, which one?"

"*Gorky Park* . . . "

"That's an old film."

"The Quay Theatre Film Club shows a lot of old films. That's why I'm a member."

"You could watch the film at home."

"I prefer to make an occasion of it. Afterwards, in the bar, we talk about the film we've just seen."

"That's nice."

"Sandra was coming with me, but she's got a cold, so I have a spare ticket."

"Are you inviting me to be your cousin's stand-in?"

"I could be."

"What time does the film start?"

"Eight o'clock . . . "

"Okay, thanks, I'll come."

"Splendid!"

Francesca looked down at the newspaper poised menacingly on the table, demanding attention.

"So, what did you want to show me?" Julian asked.

Francesca unfurled the newspaper, wrestled with it awhile as she sought the relevant page, and then laid the tabloid-sized sheets out across the table, taking care not to knock off the table either of the mugs of coffee standing stoutly before her. She folded the newspaper in half. She handed the newspaper, the lower half of page eight visible, across the table to Julian and waited expectantly for his reaction.

"Good God!" he duly exclaimed. "He's only gone and come back!"

"I thought you'd be surprised."

"I had no idea!"

"It looks like he's got himself into a spot of bother already."

"He's in hospital," Julian continued as he read the article. "The new one off the Ballingdon Road." He ran a hand through his thick black hair in exasperation. He then rubbed his cheeks and chin in the same vein. "He was involved in a road-rage incident on the Melford Road. He got into a fight. 'Mr Dewhurst, 42, and Mr Carrington, 25, remonstrated with each other before coming to blows. Mr Dewhurst suffered a fractured arm and minor head injuries, whilst Mr Carrington sustained a broken arm and a fractured skull. Neither man pressed charges against the other.' This is incredible! Even for Justin!" Julian slapped the newspaper down on the table, before adding milk and plenty of sugar to his coffee (though flustered, he did so with his usual calm deliberation) and gasping his relief at the end of the manoeuvre. "I'll go and see him after the match," he said.

"When did you last see him?"

"Six years ago, just before he left for Benidorm."

"Perhaps he's back for good?"

"A fugitive from Spanish justice, I shouldn't wonder. Most criminals from these islands go to Spain to escape British justice. Trust my brother to do it the other way around."

"Perhaps he's come back for a fresh start?"

"He went *over there* for a fresh start!"

Lizzie appeared suddenly and placed a plate of sausages, eggs and chips on the table before Julian's widened eyes. He wanted to pounce on the food and devour it, his desperation to eat—to do anything that would absorb some of his surplus nervous energy—born of both hunger and frustration with his wayward brother's latest antics. He restrained himself and managed to begin eating with a decorum commensurate with his position in society, and with a level of civility that Francesca would have expected from him.

"Well, I'd better get on," the proprietor said. "It's getting busy again."

It was true: fresh customers had entered the café and filled the remaining unoccupied tables. Lizzie was busy taking orders and, though she was calm, it was evident that she would not have objected to a helping hand.

"Thanks for letting me know about Justin, Fran," Julian said. "It's a pity that he couldn't have told me himself that he was back in town."

"Since when has your brother ever done things by the book?"

"The only books Justin's ever owned, he had to colour them in; and, even then, he used the wrong colours."

Francesca laughed, enjoying, as always, her friend's sardonic sense of humour.

"What time shall we meet this evening?" she asked.

"Half-seven? In the bar at the Quay?"

"Sounds good to me!"

"We can have a drink before the film."

"Perfect!"

Julian looked at Francesca in the way that a child looks at its mother when trying its luck to extract a concession or a favour.

"And a drink *after* the film, of course," he ventured.

"Even more perfect!"

As a lawyer mindful of the need for the rigorous use of language, Julian was minded to correct Francesca's suggestion that perfection could be improved upon, but he let the matter go. There was a time and a place for his jurisprudential pedantry, and there and then was neither.

"See you this evening," he said.

"You will!"

Even Julian's famed intellect, his cherished reason, and the rationalism that he held so dear as the only true guiding principle in life, was unable at that moment to suppress the first stirrings of an idea that was umbilically attached to romance, and he entertained the idea for that moment only, before putting it back in its box, perhaps to be indulged again another time.

THREE

Julian had to charm Sister Gabriella August into allowing him to see his brother outside official visiting hours; though he racked his brains, he was unable to recall a time when a woman had been quite so susceptible to his blandishments, or even when he had deployed such honeyed words at all. Ordinarily, he was awkward in the company of women, his speech stilted, and his posture given slowly to imploding, as if he were bent on making himself small. His newfound confidence with the ladies might have been an overflow of the euphoria engendered by the flowering of his relationship with Francesca, as if the one had cascaded joyously into the other and been carried away by it.

He found Justin sitting up in bed reading the *Daily Star*. The scene reminded him of the times when, as a boy, he would see his brother in bed immersed in the *Beano*, and he noted that the reading material had barely advanced in sophistication over the years and might even have retarded somewhat.

"Well, well, look who it isn't!"

"What are you up to?"

"I'm reading. What does it look like?"

"Allowing the words of the *Daily Star* to pass before your eyes does not constitute reading."

"You're as pompous as ever. Did you bring me any grapes?"

"Since when did you eat fruit?"

"Have you met Matron?"

"I haven't had the pleasure, no."

"Meeting her is no pleasure, I can assure you. She's a great lolloping dollop old trollop of a woman. She won't let me out of this place."

"Have a word with Ward Sister Gabriella. She's no soft touch, but with her I charmed my way *in* here, so you should be able to charm your way *out*."

"Sister Gabriella? Every time I close my eyes, I have erotic dreams about her."

"Have a word with yourself."

Julian sat down on the low armchair beside Justin's bed, and immediately found it so uncomfortable that he felt like getting back on his feet, but the effort of doing so, such was the depth to which he had sunk, would have been like ascending a hill on a child's tricycle.

"So, Justin," he began, "why all the subterfuge?"

"I don't know what that word means."

"Why did you come back without telling me?"

"I didn't want to shock you. I know how delicate you are. Anyway, you were going to find out soon enough. I can hardly hide for long in *this* town, can I?"

"I read about your roadside altercation in the *Free Press*."

"The report of the incident should have been on the front page. Page eight? I feel insulted."

"You *look* terrible."

"You should see the state of the other guy. He's over there." The patient pointed left towards the other end of the ward.

"We're mates now. We're going to meet for a beer when we get out of here."

"Get out of here? You talk as if you're in prison."

"This place *is* a bloody prison!"

"You've only yourself to blame for being here."

"Did you come here just to give me another one of your big-brother lectures?"

"No, I came here, against my better judgement, to find out what brought you back here."

"I was born here. This is my home."

"So it is," Julian said, not without sarcasm.

"Don't worry, Jules, I won't be disturbing your cosy life here. I've got things to do here, and they don't involve you."

"I'm glad to hear it."

"Though you're welcome to come to my house-warming party…"

"You've bought a house?"

Justin nodded triumphantly. He had waited a long time to get even with his brother, if only in a material sense.

"I paid cash for it."

Julian put his head in his hands, and he wanted to keep it there until the world was safe enough for him to bring it out again, which, he feared, with Justin around, would be a time long into the future.

"Are you okay?" Justin asked, revelling in the moment.

Julian peered through his splayed fingers like a fearful child watching a horror film, before asking his brother where on earth he had obtained enough cash to buy a house out-right. He then added sharply that, upon reflection, he would rather not know, and he contented himself with asking where exactly the newly acquired property was situated.

"Acton Lane," Justin replied, "with lovely views across the fields."

Julian emerged tentatively from his redoubt. "How very quaint," he said.

"It makes your flat look very pokey."

"It's big enough for me."

"Still no woman in your life then?"

"Watch this space."

"A pop group was named after your love life: the Baron Knights." The patient chuckled like a talking doll being strangled. "Hey, Sister Gabriella!" he called at the passing nurse (who was much too busy to stop and talk). "I'm a comedian! Didn't you know?"

"Your predicament is no laughing matter, Mr Di Lorenzo!" The nurse was gone.

Julian blanched at that. "Mr Di Lorenzo?" he yelled at the nurse, who by now was almost out of the ward as she ran her errands. "His name's Dewhurst!"

"My name *is* Di Lorenzo now," Justin confessed playfully, knowing that his brother would not know whether to believe him. "I changed it by deed poll ... for security reasons, you understand."

Julian's head was back in his hands. "My day has gone from the sublime to the ridiculous," he groaned. He looked out again at the world, which at that moment consisted of nothing more than his brother sitting up in a hospital bed, unshaven and unkempt, a copy of a smutty tabloid in his lap, looking nothing like his newly assumed gangster persona. He peered at Justin like a man searching the floor for a needle in the dark.

"What are you looking for?"

"The scar on your face," Julian said. "Don't gangsters have scars on their faces?"

"You doubt that I acquired my money legally?"

"Perish the thought!"

FOUR

That Saturday was an eventful day for Julian Dewhurst, one in which he learnt much about himself, and not a little about others.

He began the day by learning that even a seasoned psychoanalyst might not be able to tell him much about himself that he did not know already; further, that he himself lacked wisdom in expecting even such an eminent and renowned personage to explain a psychological negative, even when there was a perfectly functional positive with which to compare it.

That he neither liked nor understood football was reaffirmed.

He learnt that his brother was able to make a success of his life, after all, and that he himself possessed enough discretion not to enquire too deeply into how his brother had come by that success. He was bound to wonder, too, then, if he had not discovered that he was a coward in not confronting his brother about the source or sources of his newfound affluence. Discretion, he had concluded, was the better part of valour.

That his brother should have returned to his hometown so furtively had come as no surprise to him whatsoever, so there was no advance in self-knowledge from that source.

About himself, regarding Francesca, there was much new that he had gleaned, but nothing about her except that she was yet more glorious than ever he had supposed.

In the café, over lunch, she had been her usual imperiously charming self; she had beguiled simply by being herself, with not so much as a scintilla of affectation on display. During the evening, she had surpassed even her lunchtime benediction of his soul with a flawless exhibition of feminine gracefulness of thought, word and deed; never before had he felt so much himself in the company of another; so that he had barely been able to help himself when asking the question.

What had he learnt about himself in asking the question? That he was not a coward, after all, perhaps; not one to shirk a question, even when it was the hardest question he would ever have to ask.

Fortune favours the brave, it is said, and Julian that day asked himself if his entire life had not been blessed by good fortune owing to some deep reserve of bravery that seeped upwards to permeate his entire being and so govern his life.

Whatever the explanation for what and who he was, he knew that he was a truly lucky man.

FIVE

"Sister Gabriella's gunning for you!" Justin informed his brother as the two men drank beer at the bar of the Coach and Horses, round the corner from Tower Hill tube station. The pub was starting to get busy as lunchtime approached and City types drifted in, looking to unwind and relax awhile before returning to their offices to make new piles of money.

"I told you not to discharge yourself," Julian replied, "so it's *you* she should be gunning for."

"Oh, she's already given me both barrels. She's quite sexy when she's angry. I asked one of the male nurses if Sister Gabriella is single, and he told me there isn't a man brave enough to ask her out on a date."

"And you think *you're* brave enough?"

"Nothing ventured..."

"She'd eat you alive."

"Ten quid says I get a date with her."

They shook hands and sealed the bet, a bet that neither man felt confident of winning, though Julian was slightly the more confident of the two.

"Anyway," Justin said, "did you seriously expect me to stay in hospital after what you told me last night?"

"I told you that *I* was going to deal with it."

"No, this has to be something for *both* of us."

"Yes, okay," Julian conceded. "Well, you're here now, aren't you?"

"And you're sure it was *her*?"

"I'm positive."

"And you're sure she works in that big glass building across the road?"

"I've told you. On Monday morning, my tube pulled in at Tower Hill station. Her train pulled in, going in the other direction. There we were, on separate trains, but directly in line with each other, eyeing each other through two sets of windows. Her face dropped like a brick in water when she saw me. She got out of her seat, to leave the train, and, at the door, she looked back at me, you know, with fear in her eyes."

"Fear? What did she think you were going to do to her?"

"Okay, not fear, perhaps, but shock, definitely. You can imagine her surprise when she saw me."

"But how did she recognise you? It's been thirty-odd years since we last saw her. We were just kids. And how did you recognise her? She must be nearly sixty now."

"You just *do* recognise each other in these situations, don't you?"

"How did you find out where she works?"

"Yesterday morning, I took a chance. I gambled on her being at that station again, at about the same time, so I hid myself across the road somewhere, and waited, and out she came, spewing out of the Underground station, just after nine o'clock. I followed her—rather expertly, if I may say so—to the big glass building. After she'd gone inside, I waited five minutes, then I went inside myself and asked the receptionist if someone called Elaine worked for the company. 'Yes, Elaine Crawford-Menzies,' she said. I caught her totally off guard."

"Crawford-Menzies? Has she married into the aristocracy?"

"God knows."

"Aren't you supposed to be here in London for a conference this week?"

"Yes, and yesterday, on account of my amateur sleuthing, I was nearly late for my own presentation."

"What's the conference about?"

"Criminal law for the twenty-first century …"

"It sounds fascinating."

"*Criminality* for the twenty-first century is more *your* thing."

"I'm a law-abiding citizen, I'll have you know."

"Since when?"

"Look, have we got a job to do here, or what?"

"Drink up!"

Justin gulped down the remains of his beer and followed his brother out of the door and onto a London street that to him was profoundly and grotesquely alien. The capital was no place for him, as either man or transgressor. He preferred his crime petty and parochial, with the occasional foray (if the reward warranted the risk) into major expatriate villainy on the Costa Blanca.

The two men strode into the office building like two Coldstream Guardsmen marching across Horse Guards Parade to meet the Sovereign; though they were united in purpose, neither man knew what he would say once he was face-to-face with his childhood nemesis.

Julian was glad to see a different young lady from the previous day sitting on reception, because it meant that he did not have to put his planned decoy into operation; instead, he was able simply to turn a bit of charm on the new lady to forestall suspicion and so gain access to Elaine's office. He was hoping that the receptionist had no knowledge of Elaine's family history, for, though not critical, that would help in the implementation of his plan. He recalled that Elaine's only son was called Mark, and he tried to forget about the horrible little urchin even as circumstances were forcing him to remember him.

The young lady straightened her back, and adjusted her spectacles, as the two men approached. She looked as if she were seeing trouble coming.

"Good morning," Julian said to her with all the provincial savoir-faire he could muster.

"Good morning," the young lady replied, looking approvingly at the smartly dressed Julian, but somewhat dubiously at the somewhat dishevelled Justin. "Can I help you?"

"Yes, we'd like to see Elaine, please."

"Elaine Crawford-Menzies?"

Julian had to strain every sinew in trying not to laugh: from Dunkley to Crawford-Menzies, he thought, that is some conversion. "Er, yes," he stammered.

"You don't sound too sure," the receptionist said.

"Well, it's just that we can't quite get used to her new married name."

"Right," the receptionist said, her eyes narrowed in suspicion, though she was proving not to be unmoved by Julian's charm offensive. "Do you have an appointment?"

"No, we were hoping to surprise her."

"May I ask why?"

"We're her sons, you see, and it's been a while since we saw her."

"Oh, I thought she had one son and two daughters."

"That's right," Julian blundered on. "I'm her son, er, Mark, and this fine-looking chap here is her adopted son, Brian. He's literally just stepped off a plane from Australia. Hence the haggard, scruffy look."

Justin smiled at the young lady and said, "G'day!"

"Why do you want to surprise her?"

"Because today's her birthday," Julian declared confidently.

"I thought her birthday was in January."

"She's like the Queen, you see," Justin interjected. "She has an *actual* birthday and an *official* birthday."

The young lady eyed the two men as if she were a night-club bouncer and they two underage chancers trying to gain access. She had heard some flannel in her time, but these two were something else.

"It would mean *so* much to her," Julian went on with a playful insistence, hoping to God that he was not overdoing the sweet talk, "and Brian here *has* come all the way from Australia specially to surprise her."

"Okay," the receptionist said, unconvinced but just about persuaded. "You'll find her office on the third floor, at the end of the long corridor. Take this card with you. You'll need it to operate the lift."

"Thank you so much," Julian said as he snatched the card eagerly. "You've made two men very happy."

"Not for the first time, I'm sure," Justin quipped.

"I beg your pardon!"

Justin held himself back awhile as Julian strode like a man on a mission towards the lifts. He was keen to steal a few quiet words with the young lady on reception.

"My brother and I have much in common," he told her in a mock confidential tone, "except that I'm younger, cleverer and funnier than him."

"I'm pleased for you."

"We could discuss this and other matters, later, over a drink."

"I don't think so."

"You can't blame a man for trying."

In the lift, Justin challenged his brother with mad eyes and a death stare. "Brian?" he said.

"It was the first name that came into my head."

"Okay, but ... Brian?"

"Last Saturday, I got engaged."

"What?"

"Are you deaf?"

"Are you kidding me?"

"Why would I make up such a thing?"

"Who to?"

"You'll find out soon enough."

"I trust I'm invited to the wedding?"

"Of course. You're my best man."

"Oh, wow, Jules, I don't know what to say."

"There's a first time for everything."

"I feel humbled, honoured …"

"You can bring a significant other, if you can find one."

"Yes, okay, I'll bring … Who should Brian take with him to his brother's wedding? How about Mildred? Or Ethel, perhaps? No, it has to be Hilda."

"You can bring Scarlett Johansson, for all I care."

The door of the lift opened and the two men stepped out onto the long corridor. They attracted curious looks from office workers crisscrossing each other as they hurried to and from meetings. Wherever they were going, and wherever they had just been, they were all in a hurry to be elsewhere.

"We must look a right pair of berks," Justin said.

"Speak for yourself," Julian replied, and his eyes scanned himself and his brother to emphasise the difference between them in terms of presentability in a business environment.

"What are we going to say to the old witch?"

"Let's keep it respectful, Justin, shall we?"

"Oh, yes, she's only the Jezebel who wrecked our childhoods. Let's go in there and give her a big hug, shall we?"

"Let me do the talking."

"Are you sure? After the flannel you just gave that bird in reception, shouldn't you let *me* do the talking?"

"At least I didn't ask her out."

"How do you know *I* did?"

"I *know* you."

Justin held out his hand in admission of guilt. "She turned me down," he said, "but I could tell that it was a wrench for her to do so."

"I doubt she'll ever forgive herself."

"Are we going to stand here all day?"

"Follow me."

They reached the door and beheld the sign announcing: "Elaine Crawford-Menzies, Managing Director."

Julian raised his eyebrows. "She's done all right for herself," he said.

"She shagged her way up the corporate ladder, no doubt."

"Remember what I said."

"What was she doing when she lived with us?"

"She worked in a factory."

"I rest my case."

Julian knocked on the door.

"Come in!" came the woman's voice from within, and both men noticed that it was the voice they knew so well, though gravelled slightly by age.

In they went.

It was a typical modern office, barely worth describing: featureless, characterless, tasteless and soulless. Elaine was sitting in her executive chair, dressed like any other female executive, at a table fit for anyone with so grandiose a title as hers. To her left sat an obsequious-looking middle-aged man sporting a ludicrously old-fashioned moustache and a half-grown goatee beard. He looked like a cross between a new-age sage and an army sergeant-major.

Elaine was speechless, her tongue tied down by a thousand heavy-duty ropes, and her eyes widened in shock as her jaw dropped in horror. Her face was a picture that spoke a thousand words. In that moment of recognition, she was beset—besieged—by so many emotions, among them amazement and dismay, but the greatest of them was guilt. She had never supposed that there would ever be a reckoning. She had long laboured under the misapprehension that she would never see either of the Dewhurst boys again.

Two men now, they stood shoulder-to-shoulder by Elaine's desk, looking down at her, contempt and defiance in their eyes, a joint posture that visibly unnerved the woman.

"Are you okay, Elaine?" the moustachioed man asked, sounding like a knight of chivalry offering succour to a damsel in distress.

"I'm fine, thank you, Mike," the woman replied. "You may go now."

"Are you sure?"

"Yes!" she snapped.

After a quick assessment of the potential threat posed by the two intruders, Mike got up and left. The two men had certainly made an impression on him, owing principally to the stark contrast between them, the one businesslike, professional-looking, distinguished even, and the other, what with his bandages, plaster and dishevelled hair, resembling a vagabond who had just come off worse in a street brawl.

"How did you find me?"

There was no reply; indeed, there was no reply to a single word she said during the few minutes that Julian and Justin were in her room, standing before her, their eyes ablaze with scorn. Elaine would utter sentence after sentence, nervously, intimidated as she was, but no sentence would be met with a reply.

"I could say sorry, but I doubt that would be much good to you."

"I was young. I was in a very difficult situation. I lost my grip on things. What can I say?"

"Your father made matters worse. He was the worst thing that ever happened to me, and that . . . Well, for so long, there was no way out. I was trapped. The situation turned me into something of which I am now very much ashamed."

"If there's anything I can do to make it up to you, I'd be more than happy to do it."

"You two were always very different from each other. You still are, by the look of things."

"You might think that I got away with what I did without punishment. Believe me, that is not the case. Every day, I'm haunted by what happened; by what I did. My penance is a life burdened by sorrow and guilt, and a desperate wish to make amends."

"If you could see fit to forgive me, I'd be more than grateful."

"I've nothing else to say."

"Neither have I," Julian said at last. "Justin, have you anything to say?"

"No, Jules, I think you've said it all."

The brothers left the room vindicated, cleansed, and purged. They stepped into the corridor and embraced.

"You were immense in there," Justin said proudly.

"You weren't too shabby yourself."

"One for the road?"

"You took the words right out of my mouth."

Proposal

ONE

Gideon Passmore was grateful for his knowledge of the countryside around his hometown, for, though visibility in the heavy rain was poor, on officially the darkest night of the year, he knew that he was on the highway bisecting Haygreen Forest, a stretch of road that he reckoned he could navigate in his sleep.

The rain was more than heavy, it was coming down like pipes of lead out of the sky, and it was forming puddles on either side of the road that seemed determined to meet in the middle.

He had to laugh at himself, for being—evidently—the only person foolish enough to be out and about on such a filthy night, at least on that particular road. He wondered when he had last seen another car: not (he calculated) since he left the outskirts of Foxford, where he had been the guest-of-honour and keynote speaker at the annual Chamber of Commerce Christmas Dinner. He had delighted guests with his anecdotes, most of which were in deprecation of himself, and he had left the dinner, at ten minutes past ten, confident that his wit and good humour would enhance his reputation as local celebrity and pillar of the community. His one regret was that his wife had been unable to attend, for she remained if no longer stricken entirely then at least compromised. He hoped that the approaching new year would see her rehabilitation completed.

As he cruised along the highway, he pondered Jimmy's proposal of four days before, and he looked forward to being back home with his wife of two years, Georgina, who was being looked after for the evening by their neighbour and friend, Barbara. His wife was gaining in strength and courage, after her trauma of three years before, but she was still some way from being able, even tentatively, to reclaim her place in society. She needed him by her side, and he needed that need, for needing to be needed (at least by his wife) had become his greatest need.

Then he skidded to a halt after something on his left caught his eye. His bringing the car to an abrupt standstill was instinctive, and he wondered why he had done it when the thing moving was likely nothing more than a wounded animal—a deer, perhaps—for which he could have done nothing more than offer a fleeting moment of human comfort and consolation. There was enough space in the layby for him to park his car without its presence endangering passing traffic, which remained conspicuous by its absence.

Having put on the hazard-warning lights, he got out of the car and staggered in the torrential rain towards the creature, which he could see now was twitching and convulsing apparently in the throes of death. Once he was upon the unfortunate animal, he was astonished by what he saw. He was looking at no animal, no deer, but a human being, and one that he knew all too well. A thousand thoughts ran through his head in the second that it took his mind to register the pang of recognition, and he waited for the thoughts to unscramble themselves and give him something solid and cohesive upon which he might act.

The recognition was mutual.

"Gideon," the afflicted young man gasped.

"What on earth happened to you, Jimmy?" replied the other with a wicked smile, for he was enjoying the sight of his erstwhile nemesis so helpless and at his mercy. If truth be told, he was quite unable to believe his luck at finding him at his disposal, as if the gods had seen fit to answer the petitions that he had not condescended to offer them.

"Something hit me…A truck…" Jimmy wheezed, sounding like a tyre being slowly let down.

Gideon then noticed the mangled motorcycle lying a few yards away from Jimmy, and the bits of the machine that were scattered around the grass bordering the dense body of trees beyond. Unlike the motorcycle, Jimmy was still in one piece, though he looked terribly fragile, as if he would break into many pieces if someone so much as sneezed on him.

"Help me…Gideon…please…"

Gideon felt Jimmy's pockets until he found what he was looking for. He took the smartphone out of the pocket and fumbled with it in the rain, nearly dropping it in his urgency to examine its contents.

"I have the recording, Jimmy," he said gleefully.

Jimmy nodded, though such was his pain that even that simple manoeuvre was not accomplished without tremendous difficulty. Delicately, he moved his head to the left and watched as Gideon traipsed towards the forest. Gideon seemed to be standing on the edge of a precipice and peering down into it expectantly.

Proposal

"There's a ditch here, Jimmy!" Gideon called. "The water's quite deep!"

Though Jimmy knew what was about to happen, he was powerless to prevent it. He knew, too, that his entire misspent life was about to flash before his eyes like a well-known horror film on fast-forward. It would make for grim viewing.

"What if I were to roll you to the edge of this ditch here, Jimmy, and then drop you in it? How long would you last down there in the water? About fifteen seconds, I reckon. And there would be no drag marks on the grass. Anyway, the rain would wash away all trace of us."

Before Jimmy could say a word in supplication, he had been rolled to the edge of the ditch, allowed to stare down into the abyss, and then released. Even before he went down, the pain was excruciating, so many were his broken bones. He landed on his back and convulsed until he expired.

Gideon grinned in satisfaction. He saw no need to disturb the motorcycle, so he left it exactly as it was, before fleeing the scene that the police were bound to see as one where nothing more sinister than a tragic accident had occurred, albeit an avoidable one for which somebody, likely as not, would be sought for manslaughter. The beauty of the accident, as he saw it, was that it had nothing whatsoever to do with him.

His Christmas had come four days early.

TWO

In Milford, the town where he lived and worked, people were celebrating the festive season with the usual raucous revelry and debauched drunkenness. He did not enjoy Christmastime, not least because his own staff treated work as an optional extra at that time of year, so that one entire month and more of his company's time became a stranger to productivity. If he had his way, Christmas would be abolished and the public holidays of the season replaced with memorials to something more rational, though he had little or no idea as to what. The winter solstice, he thought: at least it is known to exist.

He was leaning on a railing on the quay, by the theatre, looking out across the river, which glinted like shards of watery glass under the multi-coloured glowing lamps. For a second, he was dazzled by it all, and after looking away he had to squint to regain his focus.

A man in a designer suit walked past him with a woman on each arm, the one a blonde and the other a brunette. The two women wore dresses that were designed more for July than December.

"Want to join us?" the blonde called out to Gideon, trying to be seductive but sounding merely pornographic, as she and her prospective companions for the night headed towards the executive apartments at the far end of the quay.

Gideon watched them go by, the women's backsides gyrating in the way he so hated when the "fairer sex" was comporting itself in an overtly sexual manner. Given the choice between having sex with the two women, alluring physically though they were, and drowning them in the river, he would have chosen the latter option, all day long. They were tarts at Christmastime, and they were tarts at every other time of the year. Given what he was prone to witnessing, daily, how could he have thought anything to the contrary? The man was bound to unwrap two Christmas presents, four days early, and he was welcome to them. Even before meeting his wife, Georgina, he had been faithful to her. He despised men who could not be true to their wives, even their future wives. The man in the designer suit deserved death by drowning even more than the two women.

Gideon fumbled with Jimmy's phone until he found the infamous recording. He played some of it. He smiled at the memory of the interview, but he winced too. He deleted the recording, just in case. He took one more look around him before launching the instrument into the river. That sealed it. He was safe as houses. He and Georgina were now free to live their life together without threat from a scoundrel. He was free to continue nurturing the one and only true love of his life. His dirty secret was resting at the bottom of the river, it was lying in a ditch, broken, and drowned, never to see the light of day again.

"Goodbye, Jimmy," he said.

He would go home to his wife now, happy in the knowledge that nobody and nothing foreseeable could snatch away from him and his beloved their domestic idyll, something which both had long coveted, and which they would never surrender now that they had found it.

He had found happiness. He would have killed to maintain it.

His wife's happiness was simply an extension of his own.

THREE

He arrived home to find Barbara and Georgina laughing, and the spent bottle of claret and two empty glasses on the coffee-table confessing eloquently their part in creating (for Gideon) such a heart-warming and uplifting scene.

Barbara was a lively woman ideal for the task of keeping Georgina occupied whenever Gideon had to be out on business, and her being fifteen years his wife's senior was no barrier to her routinely carrying out the task with aplomb. Not that keeping Georgina company was any kind of chore for their neighbour, for she was a lonesome spinster and so appreciated the company herself.

"You two look like you've been having a good time," Gideon said, seeing straightaway that both women had noticed the state he was in, not that they could have failed to notice.

Barbara stood up and approached Gideon, cautiously, as if he were not quite the person she had expected to see, and she searched him, curiously, not quite able to believe her eyes. He had left the house immaculate and had returned looking like a scarecrow.

Gideon often looked at Barbara in the same way that she looked at him now, for she had (to put it politely) an eccentric dress sense: that evening, she wore green slacks with an orange turtleneck sweater, an effect that was spared complete ignominy by a pair of trendy-looking black boots. He could not remember the colour of her coat, but he guessed that it was purple, and, in a spirit of masochistic inquisitiveness, he looked forward to seeing it.

"What the dickens happened to you, sweetheart?" Barbara trilled. She called everyone she met "sweetheart".

"I was driving through Haygreen Forest when I desperately needed a pee," Gideon replied. "When I got out of the car, I went over to some trees, slipped in the mud, and fell over."

"Too much booze, huh?" Barbara wondered cheekily.

"Nothing but orange juice, water and coffee has passed my lips this evening, but I see that you two really *have* been drinking."

"To be fair, *I* drank most of it, reprobate that I am," Barbara admitted. "Georgie has been as good as gold."

"You can drink as much as you like," Gideon replied. "You've only to stagger next door, after all."

"Oh, but I have to get up early tomorrow morning to finish my Christmas shopping."

"Best we don't open another bottle then," Gideon said.

"I should be going," Barbara announced. "I'll leave you two lovebirds in peace."

"You don't have to rush off," Gideon said, hoping that she would.

"No, really, I have to get my head down."

"Okay, well, thanks for keeping Georgie company this evening. It's much appreciated."

"Thanks, Barbara," Georgina said from her comfortable redoubt on the sofa. "Will you come round on Christmas morning for a sherry?"

"I'd be delighted."

Georgina got to her feet and, with her husband, escorted Barbara to the hallway, where Gideon helped open Barbara's (turquoise) coat for her to slip into.

"Thanks again," Gideon said.

"The pleasure was all mine."

When Gideon opened the front door, a shower of rain was blown in by the strong wind, spraying the faces of all three people standing in the elaborately furnished hallway. The rain had relented considerably, from the torrential to mere drizzle, but the wind had got up to compensate for the diminished precipitation.

"The rain's eased up, I see," Gideon said. "You won't get wet."

"No, but I might be blown away," Barbara laughed, before stepping gingerly into the night and hurrying up the driveway, at the top of which she turned left, before turning left again into her own driveway.

"Eleven o'clock! Christmas morning!" Gideon called, whereupon Barbara raised a hand in agreement, a gesture that became a wave just before she put her key in the front door and disappeared from view.

Gideon closed his front door behind him and then embraced his wife. "So, you had a nice evening?" he asked her.

Georgina nodded. She smiled. "It was a lovely evening," she said. "Barbara's such good company."

"We're lucky to have her as a neighbour."

"And a friend…"

"We could go for a walk on Christmas Day, after lunch?"

"I'm not sure, love," Georgina sighed back, her face screwed up in anguish. "I'm not sure I'm ready yet."

"Of course, you must take your time."

"I know it's been three years since…and more than two years since my breakdown…But I'm getting there. Give it just a few more weeks and I'll be ready."

"We could go out in the car first, out into the country, away from the city. We could have a pub lunch somewhere."

Georgina nodded but without conviction. She was a long way from being ready to live a normal life again, the first step towards the attainment of which would be the first step taken outside her sanctuary, the marital home, the only place where she felt remotely safe. They both knew that. They were trying to take each day at a time.

"Fancy a nightcap?"

Georgina nodded, eager to please her husband in some small way. "Sure," she said. "Why not?"

Gideon held Georgina tight to him and kissed her on the forehead. "We're untouchable now," he declared. "Safe as houses."

Surprised by his vehement tone, Georgina moved her face away from her husband's. He winked at her and so allayed her suspicion—her fear—that his impassioned words had been born of frustration—anger even—at her continued inability to face the world at large.

He led her back into the living-room, where she resumed her place on the sofa. She had to laugh at him as he poured two brandies over by the drinks cabinet.

He noticed her tittering to herself and, with so much love that his heart almost burst, asked her what was so funny.

"Look at the state of you!" She laughed again.

He looked down at himself and saw a suit and shoes caked in mud. "Oh, yes, what a mess. I'll go and get changed. I'll take the suit to the drycleaner's tomorrow."

He put the drinks on the coffee-table, and then proceeded upstairs, leaving her wondering what she had done to deserve such a loving and caring man for a husband; a man who would do anything, absolutely anything, for her; a man who would die for her; a man who, if he had to, she felt sure, would *kill* for her.

FOUR

Four days previously—so, eight days before Christmas—Gideon was entertaining clients in a wine bar when he had the shock of his life, when the last person he would have expected to see bustled into the busy establishment, incongruous for being a hoodie amid the glinting chrome and glass, and made for him as if he had known he would be there. It was lunchtime, and Gideon was being made to reflect that never had he seen such a promising lunch wrecked so precipitously and with such reckless disregard for business proprieties.

Knowing that he would have to engage with the intruder, he made his excuses, got to his feet, and met his would-be nemesis head-on, swallowing hard in anticipation of a fraught encounter.

"Hello, Gideon," the young man said, his words a threat dressed up as a greeting, but dressed so badly that they were barely recognised as a greeting at all.

"What are you doing here, Jimmy?"

"I came out of the nick only this morning, Gideon. Did nobody tell you? Or did you think I'd gone inside for life?"

"Outside!" Gideon said firmly, trying to assume control of the situation. "Out the back!"

Once they were outside, surrounded by bins overflowing with the festering remains of several days' worth of lunches, Jimmy lit a cigarette and gasped in relief. It was his first cigarette since his reacquaintance with freedom had begun.

"How did you know I was here?" Gideon pressed Jimmy, still striving for control.

"I have my sources, Gideon. I've known your every move since I went inside. My eyes and ears are everywhere."

"Who do you think you are? Don Corleone? A couple of years inside and you come out acting like a gangster?"

"Let's not argue, Gideon?"

The two men could not have looked more different: the elder, immaculately groomed and attired; the other, a mess of straggly, greasy hair, soiled jeans, and scruffy hooded top.

"This place used to be a decent boozer," Jimmy said, resuming his offensive. "What was it called? The Olive Branch, wasn't it? Now look at it. Oranges! A bloody wine bar! This town is selling its soul."

To Gideon's consternation, Jimmy had started hopping around, moving from foot to foot, with a nervous restlessness, which (Gideon knew) Jimmy did when he was agitated, or just plain angry.

"What do you want, Jimmy?"

"Justice, Gideon. I want justice."

"Don't you come to me, calling the shots. We're quits."

"Oh, we're quits, are we?"

"That's what I said."

"How do you work that out?"

"We had a deal. I honoured my side of the bargain, and so did you, only you messed up your bit."

"Messed it up? You told me that hardly anyone walked along that towpath, so that, if I jumped that woman, nobody would notice. You paid me to jump her after dark, when, you said, the towpath would be *deserted*."

"It *was* deserted."

"So, how come two blokes came after me? How come I spent two-and-a-half years inside for attempted rape? How come I've now got a criminal record and no chance of getting a job?"

"You weren't quick enough. It should have been a fifteen-second job. You were supposed to *pretend* to jump her and sexually assault her, and I was supposed to *pretend* to fight you off, then you were supposed to *pretend* to overpower me and run away, but I found myself *actually* fighting you off, because you seemed to be *actually* trying to rape her, so that you had *actually* to overpower me. All that took so bloody long that two men came upon the scene, you legged it, and they went in hot pursuit of you and quickly caught up with you. That's why the plan went tits up. Blame yourself, Jimmy. Anyway, I paid you in advance, so you've still got the money. That should help you set yourself up somewhere."

"I came out of this five grand richer, agreed, but in every other way I got the shit end of the stick, while you got yourself a lovely new wife and got to play the hero. Honestly, you couldn't make it up."

"Don't forget where you were when I found you, Jimmy. You were in the gutter. You'd spent much of your childhood in borstal, and you'd just come out of the slammer, with little hope and no prospects. Even your family had disowned you, and there's no danger of any of them being canonised anytime soon. I gave you a job. I put you back on your feet. I gave you a chance."

"And now I'm back in the gutter, thanks to you!"

"Because *you* screwed up, Jimmy!"

"Because *you* put me up to it, Gideon!"

"And *you* agreed to do it, Jimmy!"

"Because *you* told *me* that nothing could possibly go wrong, Gideon!"

For a minute or so, neither man spoke. Jimmy stubbed out his cigarette on the ground with the firm heel of a hefty boot, and began hopping from foot to foot again, more agitated than cold. He approached Gideon and eyeballed him menacingly.

"I was going straight. I had my life in order for the first time—yes, I accept, all thanks to you—but, also thanks to you, I'm back to square one. Actually, I'm a lot *worse off* than I was before you came to my rescue."

"We've been over this, Jimmy."

Jimmy took a step back from Gideon, an act that was not seen by the latter as in any way conciliatory, since the former's eyes remained ablaze with anger.

"I could make life very difficult for you, Gideon. In fact, I could ruin you."

"How do you figure that?"

"I could blow down the ear of your good lady wife."

"You'd have a job. She hasn't left the house since we got married. After the attack, she was fine for a while. Then we married. Then she suffered a nervous breakdown, from which she has not yet fully recovered."

"It sounds like your little plan has backfired more times than one of Boycie's second-hand motors."

"I'm not unhappy with how things have turned out."

"That's because you got what you wanted, Gideon, and more!"

"Not exactly!"

Jimmy began to circle Gideon with a menacing sneer playing across his face. He was like a vulture sensing an opportunity to partake of a small indulgence.

"Of course, I could go to the police and tell them the *full* story."

"You could have done that three years ago, Jimmy, after they'd arrested you. You could have revealed all at the trial. The police wouldn't have believed you then, and they certainly won't believe you now. Your word against mine? A serial offender's word against that of a respected businessman and pillar of the community? You haven't thought this through, have you, Jimmy?"

"I did three years' bird for you, Gideon, and don't you forget it!"

"You didn't do three years' bird for me, Jimmy, for the simple reason that you couldn't have told the police the full story, even if you'd wanted to. You had no proof."

Jimmy sniggered to himself. He looked gleeful, as if the woman of his dreams had just accepted his proposal of marriage. As if he were about to produce a diamond ring from his jacket pocket, ready to brandish at his betrothed, he reached inside and slowly pulled out a mobile phone, an innocent enough manoeuvre, ordinarily, that had the watching Gideon trembling with a sense of foreboding. Jimmy pressed a few buttons, held out the phone at arm's length, and treated Gideon to a recorded excerpt of their infamous dialogue, when a proposal of a type wholly different from marriage was made. Jimmy played only the first thirty seconds or so of the exchange, but it was enough to alert Gideon to the fact that the entire conversation had been recorded for posterity.

"I taught you well, Jimmy," Gideon said. "How resourceful you've become."

"I'd been shafted too many times not to give myself some insurance, my friend. When you summoned me to the pub that night, I knew you were up to something. You can't kid a kidder. So, I made sure I got the interview recorded. And aren't I glad I did? The sound quality isn't perfect—the phone *was* in my coat pocket when I made the recording, after all—but it's good enough … and, anyway, the police, with all their gadgets, can do all sorts of things to improve the quality of a recording, so I've no worries on that count."

"So, you have a recording of our conversation of three years ago. What are you planning to do with it?"

"You owe me, Gideon. If you slip me another five grand, I'll delete the recording and move on to another town. I'm moving on, anyway, but I'd rather move on without any unpleasantness between us, and it would be such a shame if you lost your good lady wife *and* had to spend time inside. Prison would chew up someone like you and spit you out, my friend."

"I'll have to think about your proposal, Jimmy. I'm a businessman. I'm not in the habit of accepting proposals without thinking about them."

"You've got seven days, Gideon."

"That takes us to Christmas Eve."

"Have you got a problem with that?"

"I was planning on spending Christmas Eve with my wife."

"Then you'll just have to make your excuses and leave her for an hour or so, won't you?"

"Where?"

"In the Flying Horses, where this whole sorry episode began. One o'clock. Lunchtime. I want the money in cash. If you're not there, well, you know what the consequences will be."

"If I give you the money, you move on, and I never see your ugly mug again." Gideon's gaze was fixed on Jimmy with a rare intensity. "Understood?"

"We understand each other perfectly, Gideon."

"Get out of my sight, Jimmy."

"Until this time next week, then, Gideon …"

"Don't bank on it."

"You'll be there, Gideon. You're no fool."

Jimmy was the first to go back into the bar (as he made his way out, via the front door), and Gideon was left standing there, rooted to the spot, humiliated, seething with resentment, his mind working feverishly as it strove to formulate a scheme, a course of action, anything, that would forestall his giving so much as a penny to a man whom he believed he owed nothing: nothing, perhaps, except for a lesson in how not to cross someone way out of his league.

FIVE

Three years previously (it was on the sixth day of December), Gideon and Jimmy were sitting in the (relatively quiet) corner of a noisy pub, the Flying Horses, locked in a strained dialogue that was not made easier by the consumption of strong Belgian beer.

Gideon had summoned Jimmy, and Jimmy was keen to know why.

"Okay, Gideon, that's enough small talk," Jimmy said with all the respect he felt he owed his mentor and (he had to concede, for it was not too strong a word) saviour. "Why have you brought me here?"

"Am I not allowed to have a drink with my old friend?"

"What's so important that we couldn't talk about it in the office?"

"I want to run something past you, Jimmy."

"Is it work-related?"

"I'd be lying if I said it was."

Jimmy held out his arms as if he were about to fly away. "I'm listening," he declared.

"I want you to do me a favour, Jimmy."

"I don't like the sound of this, Gideon."

"Hear me out, Jimmy."

"Like I said, Gideon, I'm listening."

Gideon braced himself with a deep intake of breath: he had quite a speech to make, and it was important that he pitched it just right.

"I'm going to make you a proposal, Jimmy, but you mustn't see it as a quid pro quo."

"I don't even know what that means."

"You don't owe me anything, Jimmy."

"You're talking in riddles, Gideon."

"It would be fair to say that I've helped you get your life back on track, wouldn't it?"

"More than fair…"

"When you came out of prison, your life was as good as over. You didn't have a friend in the world. You had no chance of finding work. Even your family had turned its back on you. Yet, I, Gideon Passmore, saw something in you. I'd heard about you. I'd followed you from afar. Well, you know, insofar as 'afar' is applicable in this crummy little town."

Jimmy sighed his impatience and downed some Leffe.

"I'm a peerless judge of character, Jimmy. I saw through the person the rest of the world saw. I saw through all that, to the person you *are*. I saw the real Jimmy Johnson. I saw that you had been failed by society, Jimmy, and that you had been let down by your own family, the very people who have now so cruelly and abjectly cast you aside. I saw what you had to offer if only someone would take a chance on you, show some faith in you, put his arm around you and allow you to make a go of things, to prove your worth. And now look at you, Jimmy, three years later. You've gone from postboy to manager of the post room, which, thanks to you, runs like clockwork. There's not a single person in the company who's thought of more highly than you are, Jimmy. You have justified—*totally* justified—my faith in you."

Jimmy allowed the blizzard of words to settle in his mind before responding. He took a deep breath. He drank some more strong Belgian beer. Then he spoke.

"I appreciate what you say, Gideon, really, I do, but I *have* heard it all before."

"It bears repeating, Jimmy."

"And you don't have to make excuses for me, Gideon. Don't blame society. Don't blame my family. *I* made the decisions that put me in jail, not them. It's all about character. I changed. I came out of prison determined, somehow, to put myself on the straight and narrow, and, with your help, I've managed to do that. We all have the same choices in life, Gideon."

"That's what I like about you, Jimmy: your sense of personal responsibility. That's what sets you apart from the crowd."

"What's this all about, Gideon?"

"Oh, yes, well . . . Bear in mind that you're perfectly entitled to say no to what I'm about to propose."

"Why have I got a bad feeling about all this?"

"I want you to attack someone."

Jimmy spluttered on his beer, nearly choking on it as he took in Gideon's words. He was not sure that he had heard right his friend and mentor. One of them was losing the plot and he was as sure as he could be that it was not himself.

"What?"

"You heard me, Jimmy."

"Have you lost your mind?"

"I want you to *pretend* to attack someone."

"I don't believe I'm hearing this."

"Listen to me. You know that my office looks out over the old canal towpath, don't you?"

"I do."

"Well, every day, every *week*day, at about four o'clock in the afternoon, this woman—she's bewitchingly beautiful—walks along the towpath. I see her."

"Nobody walks along that towpath anymore. It doesn't lead anywhere."

"Georgina does!"

"You're on first-name terms with her, then, are you?"

Gideon nodded enthusiastically, eager to get his story out now that he had started telling it.

"A couple of days ago, on the towpath, I bumped into her—accidentally on purpose, of course—and we got talking. It turns out that her mother lives on the other end of the towpath, and that Georgina goes to see her every day."

"There's nothing at the other end of the towpath. All the houses over that way were knocked down to make way for the new flyover."

"All the houses except one, Jimmy."

Jimmy shot Gideon with a quizzical look.

"There's one house standing in splendid isolation, in the middle of what is now wasteland. It looks rather vulnerable, I imagine, especially with the Chapeltown Estate nearby. That house belongs to Georgina's mother. She refused to budge when the compulsory-purchase order was made. She'll be ousted eventually, of course, but you have to admire her for standing her ground."

"She's a fool."

"The house has been in her family for generations. She was born in the house, as was Georgina. They will take it over her dead body."

"Sounds like it will come to that."

"She will be forcibly removed, and the house will be flattened. Even Georgina's redoubtable old mother cannot stand in the way of progress."

Jimmy shook his head. "Some progress!" he exclaimed.

"Anyway," Gideon went on, keen to steer the conversation back on course, "I intercepted Georgina on the towpath, the day before yesterday, making it look like I was casually strolling by, and we talked."

"You approached her from the other end of the towpath?"

"No, I was hiding in the bushes on the towpath, those opposite the company building."

Jimmy shook his head in disbelief.

"And then I simply emerged out of the gloom and appeared before her. It was gloomy. It wasn't difficult to make it look like I'd come from the other end of the towpath."

"I've pulled a few strokes in my time, Gideon, but nothing like this."

"During our little chat, I gleaned all the information I needed: why she walks along the towpath every day at four o'clock; where she lives; where she works; and, most importantly of all, whether she's single."

"*Is* she single?"

"Of course, she is! If she weren't, do you think we'd be plotting this little caper?"

"*You're* plotting, Gideon, not *me*!" Jimmy gulped down some beer as if his life depended on it. "So, the idea is that I attack this Georgina woman, or *pretend* to, and you come along and fight me off, or *pretend* to, I have it away on my toes, you're the hero, and you get the girl?"

"You've named that tune in one, Jimmy!"

"Why all the cloak-and-dagger stuff, Gideon? You're loaded. You'd be a good catch. You could get it together with her in the normal way."

Gideon shook his head. "No, Jimmy, she's way out of my league, and she's not the kind of woman to marry a man for his money."

"You talk as if you know the woman."

"I've looked into her eyes, Jimmy. I *know*."

"Have you been taking drugs?"

"Jimmy, come on, get real."

Jimmy looked at Gideon as if his friend and boss had suddenly metamorphosed into a giant bug. It was a look of astonishment with a hint of disgust.

"I'm not doing it," Jimmy announced, his voice as firm as a schoolmaster's when meting out detention to a recalcitrant child.

"Lost your bottle, have you, Jimmy?"

"I'm going straight!"

"You'll still be going straight, Jimmy. What can possibly go wrong? Trust me. All you have to do is hide in the same bush I hid in, jump on Georgina as she passes—be gentle, though—fight me off when I jump on you, and leg it. It's beautifully simple."

"What if she gets a good look at me?"

"She won't. The towpath is dimly lit, as you know, and, anyway, it will all happen too quickly for her to register what's happening. She won't have a clue."

"What's in it for me?"

"Five-thousand pounds, cash in hand, up front . . . "

Jimmy was no great thinker, but the cogs in his brain were soon turning with such urgency that his grey matter was in danger of overheating. It was not so much that he found the money a seductive prospect, more a case of his suddenly having to re-evaluate the extent of his commitment to remaining implacably on the straight and narrow. He knew who he had been, and he knew who he had become, but who would he be tomorrow, and the day after tomorrow?

"I need to think about this, Gideon?"

"There's no time for that, Jimmy!"

"No?"
"We need to move on this."
"When?"
"Tomorrow!"

The Long Eclipse

It was the first day without daylight, the previous such day having come the day before, and the next such day, the next such *first* day, coming the day after. Every day was the first day without daylight.

How such a day had come about is not important, or at least not worth discussing. Suffice it to say that it simply was; and how and why it remained so is beyond the scope of this story.

The streets, deprived of daylight, were grim and austere in their utter bleakness, and depended for such illumination as they had on the few streetlamps that continued to work. There were dark corners, there were darker corners still, and there were corners too dark to be identifiable as corners at all. There were black holes, and there was simple blackness, a vast wall of a colour too dark to be seen.

Nobody in that place, at that time, had known any different, or, if they had, they had barely any recollection of it.

It was a time that time had forgotten.

It was a place where nobody before had lived, not even the people who lived there now.

Darkness, somehow, had descended.

Somehow, the light had never returned.

When Oswald woke up, it was dark. Of course, it was dark. His head was aching after the dreams. He had only a vague idea what he was going to do that day. He had no work to do that day, and it was difficult to distinguish one day from another when there was no beginning and no end to darkness. Slowly, the recollection of a plan formed in his mind.

Like everyone else of working age, he worked an on-off shift pattern, one week on and one week off, working alternate weekends. People worked in "essential" industries only, there being no what used to be known as "champagne-bubble companies" to provide gainful employment; no "here today and gone tomorrow" non-jobs; no jobs that did not need to be done and that had *never* needed to be done; no jobs, that is, serving mere human vanity and the wish to make money for the sake of making money. Oswald worked at a power station, in a menial capacity, though he was paid the same as everyone else not only in the power station itself but also in the country at large. That is how it was: every working person was paid the same amount of money by the state, and the amount of money paid, though barely above subsistence level, was enough for what people needed. As the state told the people, again and again, they were paid as much money as they needed, and they would be forever happy. There was no question of the people buying what they "liked", since such things no longer existed; and, in any case, nobody alive could remember a time when such things *had* existed.

Oswald staggered out of bed, his blond hair adhering to his head in places but generally in a state of anarchy. He yawned. He looked down at himself and noticed that he was wearing pyjamas. He wondered how that had happened. He needed to go to the bathroom to relieve himself, but he could hear the voices of Adrian and his four friends coming from the kitchen, and he had to walk past the kitchen to get to the bathroom, so he was bound to be seen. Adrian was all right, but Oswald was wary of his four friends because there was something insidiously menacing about them, like dogs that bared their teeth and growled without either barking or biting. Adrian was the official householder of the apartment. The four friends simply occupied the place much of the time, drinking vodka and playing cards, filling the place with their boorish jokes and raucous laughter, and casting looks of suspicion over Oswald whenever their paths crossed.

Oswald was registered as living at the apartment; before moving there, he had lived in an orphanage, but Adrian took him in after Oswald had lied to the police for him to give him an alibi; though the police remained convinced that Adrian had committed the crime, they were unable to prove it, thanks to Oswald's intervention.

Oswald stepped out onto the landing and immediately five heads turned to face him. The five men were drinking coffee, though shortly they would be drinking vodka. They would drink and play cards. Supposedly, they all had jobs, though Oswald saw precious little evidence of gainful employment in their ranks. They stared at him as if he were an apparition from another place, a visitation from another dimension, and as if, despite his apparent foreignness, they could not be bothered to think about him and why he had manifested himself to them.

Oswald was stupefied by the attention, not least that of the four visitors, any one of whom he would have crossed the road to avoid.

"You have a message, Oswald," Adrian announced in the tone of the patrician. "It came through on the teleprinter. It's from Sonia. She said she'll meet you in Jim's Café at eleven."

"What's the time now?" Oswald asked, glad of the chance to speak now that he had been spoken to.

"Nine-thirty," Adrian replied.

"Thanks for taking the message," Oswald said. He looked at each of the four men in turn, quite unable to judge which of them looked the most disagreeable. Each one of them looked as though he would kill his own mother in cold blood. Oswald could not fathom what Adrian saw in them as friends. Adrian was decent, all things considered. These men were not.

"It was no problem," Adrian said, again in a fatherly tone. "The message just came through, so I took it."

"Well," Oswald said awkwardly, "thanks all the same."

Oswald was glad to reach the sanctuary of the bathroom.

Oswald and Sonia sat in Jim's Café, gazing at each other across two cups of steaming-hot coffee. The café was lit by lamps which glowed here and there like little beacons of burnished gold. Light was a precious commodity, not one to be wasted, and Jim used it as sparingly as anyone.

The café was situated next to a warehouse that had once been a church. Nobody could have cared less about that.

"Were the four men at the flat this morning?" Sonia asked, her eyes sympathising like those of a mother brooding over a troubled child.

"They're *always* at the flat," Oswald responded with a deep sigh of resignation.

"Are you going to see the old man today?" Sonia enquired of her friend.

"Yes . . ."

"And the old lady?"

"Yes . . ."

"Who is the old man?"

"I don't know."

"Who is the old woman?"

"I don't know."

"Where did you meet them?"

"I don't know."

Sonia withdrew from Oswald for a moment, sensing his mood, which made Oswald feel guilty for upsetting his friend, his close friend, his only friend in the world other than Adrian, and he was more of a father figure than a friend. As for his real father, not to mention his real mother: what had happened to them? He knew nothing about them. They were not strangers to him. They had simply never existed. He toyed with the idea that he was not the product of an act of procreation at all, but instead had simply emerged from the all-pervading darkness, a gathering apparition, a manifestation of the eternal night.

"I'm sorry, Sonia," he said sharply. "I'm always a bit edgy before I visit the old man and the old lady."

"Why do you visit them?"

"I'm drawn to them."

"I don't understand."

"Neither do I."

Sonia gambled on her coffee now being cool enough from which to take a sip; and, when she did so, Oswald followed suit.

"Oswald?" she said.

"Yes," he replied, eagerly, and he leaned forward a little to receive her word.

"You said that the old man and the old lady are sinister."

"Well, the old lady is sinister, for sure, but the old man is almost likeable."

"Do they live far apart?"

"It's hard to tell," Oswald sighed. "It's so dark."

"Tell me something more about them."

"I'd rather not."

"Please!"

Oswald sighed again and winced as he prepared to tell his friend what little he knew about the elderly pair: they were almost as much a mystery to him as they were to her.

"They look strangely familiar. It's hard to describe. And I sense that they *know* each other; or *knew* each other; that they were *married* even."

"To each other?"

"Yes…"

"That's really something!"

"I've asked both of them if they've ever been married, and they both refuse to answer the question. Whenever I ask them the question, they look like they've seen a ghost."

"How old are they exactly?"

"Between seventy and eighty, though closer to eighty, I would guess."

"They're pretty old then."

"But, you know, it's weird, I can't help thinking that I'm seeing them not as they *are*, but as they *will* be, you know, sometime in the future. They don't seem quite real to me. And, when I'm with them, I don't feel *myself* either. I don't feel real. I feel like a copy of myself: identical, but not the same."

"We're *all* copies of someone, Oswald."

"Of the *same* someone?"

"No, I mean that I'm a copy of someone and you're a copy of someone else."

"So, the person of whom I'm a copy is also *my* copy?"

"Yes…"

"A double?"

"Not a double, but a copy…"

"What's the difference?"

"There's all the difference in the world."

Oswald shook his head rather than give the matter any further thought. He wondered if Sonia's exposition had been seriously considered or put forward as a joke.

"Do you know their names?"

Oswald shook his head again. "I've never asked them," he replied.

"Do they know *your* name?"

Again, the shake of the head. "They've never asked."

"Ask them, today, when you see them."

"Today, what's said—between me and him, and then between me and her—will be exactly the same as what's said between us every other day."

"So, vary the conversation."

"I can't."

"Why not?"

"It's not possible. You know how it is."

"I do."

"It's all so difficult to understand: the old man, the old lady, Adrian, and his four friends. But you, Sonia, I understand that. Because you're not like everything and everyone else. You are wholesome. You are the only wholesome thing in my life."

"Oh, so I'm a *thing* now, am I?" She smiled to show her friend that her woundedness had been a pretence.

"You know what I mean."

"I do."

She placed a hand on his and smiled warmly at him. It was just what he needed. It was just what *she* needed. She thought about asking if she might accompany Oswald on his visits to the old man and the old lady, but she quickly dismissed the idea as unworkable, for she knew that he would never agree to it: seeing the old man and the old lady was something he had to do alone.

"What time will you finish your visits?"

"About six..."

"Shall we meet here at six-thirty?"

"Sure..."

They finished their drinks in silence.

The old lady's house was so dark that she and Oswald could barely see each other as they talked. The conversation was stilted and, when it flowed, it was only slightly less stilted. Above all, the conversation was aimless, like an arrow without a target.

"Who are you, son?" the old lady asked Oswald.

He saw the face glowing in the light given by the lamp beside her, but the rest of her was a shadow trying hard to be a silhouette.

"Why do you call me 'son'?"

"Because you've always looked strangely familiar to me..."

"So have you to me, but I don't call you 'mother'."

"How did we meet, son?"

"I don't remember. What does it matter? We met. I'm here."

Earlier that day, he had had the very same conversation with the old man, in another place, but in the same dark place.

"Who are you, son?"

"Why do you call me 'son'?"

"Because you've always looked strangely familiar to me..."

"So have you to me, but I don't call you 'father'."

"How did we meet, son?"

"I don't remember. What does it matter? We met. I'm here."

The old lady asked Oswald if he would retrieve for her an old tablecloth from the chest of drawers in the corner of the room: she wished to make tea for two, with a nice spread of crockery, and she wanted her best tablecloth for the occasion.

Oswald had to move carefully towards the chest of drawers as the old lady's living-room was cluttered with furniture that barred his way; when, eventually, he reached the drawers, he awaited further instructions.

"It's in the top drawer, son," the old lady said in her usual breathless, squawking tone. "Turn the lamp on if you need to."

"It's okay," Oswald said. "I'm used to looking for things in the dark."

Oswald opened the top drawer and the first thing he saw inside it was not a tablecloth but a framed photograph of a young man and a young woman on their wedding day. They, too, looked strangely familiar to him. He held out the photograph, held it towards what little light there was in the room, and peered at it with almost loving reverence; almost, indeed, with longing. His heart raced as his eyes lingered on the image. As the photograph held his rapt attention, Oswald tried hard to resist its magnetic power; but it was hopeless, since the force, once static and immediate, pulled him inwards, into the depths of the photograph, into the past, and bade him follow the couple to an outlandish place situated in another time.

Or did they step out of the photograph so that he was drawn to follow them?

Whichever it was, the upshot was that he found himself in a place full of light and air and strange, unfamiliar sounds such as trilling and tweeting and sundry other expressions of joy and rapture. A surge of happiness went through his body at the same time as a sense of alienation overcame and almost overpowered him. What I describe is a commonplace scene; but, for Oswald, he might as well have been on the moon; in fact, the moon would have seemed a less alien place to him.

As he followed the couple from the photograph around the new place, he could see them, obviously, but they, apparently, were unable to see him. He was to them invisible.

The man stepped out of a country pub, holding a pint of beer, and, as Oswald had upon finding himself in this new place, squinted as his eyes made the adjustment from the darkness of the public house to the bright light of the garden outside. He looked around the garden and saw that every trestle table was occupied by people with backpacks; every table, that was, except one, at which sat a lone woman of about his age. He saw plenty of space at her table for a man to sit. He saw, too, an opportunity. He approached the table with due regard for the woman's personal space.

"Good morning," he said, trying to sound diffident but sounding, instead, rather confident.

The woman looked up at him benignly. "It's *afternoon*," she said politely.

He looked at his watch. "So it is," he returned, feeling at once foolish and glad of the mistake for enabling his opening conversational gambit. "May I?" he said with a nod at the seat opposite the woman.

"Be my guest," she said.

He disliked trestle tables for always being so difficult to sit at: nobody, he thought, should have to embark upon a climbing operation just to take a seat at a table. He placed his beer on the table and observed that the woman was drinking something devoid of alcohol, orange juice with lemonade, possibly, from a half-pint glass.

"Lovely time of year, May, isn't it?" he said. "Chaucer wasn't wrong: 'Hard is the heart that loveth nought in May.' Sorry, I'm rambling."

"Isn't that why you're here? To ramble?"

The man chuckled, his heart warmed by the woman's witticism.

"Well, yes," he said.

The woman studied him as she sipped from her glass.

"I don't often do this, you know," he said.

"What? Talk to strange women in remote country pubs?"

"No, I mean, walking in the country. I'm a city man. I don't understand the countryside. All the sounds and smells are alien to me. And the sights! I look around and all I see is trees and grass and fields. It's the randomness of it all that gets me. Take that tree over there. Why is it there and not over there? Why is it where it is? When I see a building in the city, I know it's where it is because someone decided to put it there. There is logic, reason, behind it. The only thing I understand out in the country is pubs. So, that's what I do out in the country: I wander, lonely as a cloud, from one pub to another."

The woman took some time to absorb the man's monologue, before smiling to herself, almost as if to patronise him rather than to indulge him, still less to engage with him.

"The next pub's five miles up the track," she declared eventually.

The man smiled and seized the moment to make a little joke. "Well," he said, lifting his pint of beer, "I can walk off this then."

There was silence between them for about a minute as the conversation had run out, worryingly quickly for both, and as looking around and admiring the beautiful scenery seemed a more rewarding way to pass the time than talking.

Eventually, their eyes met again, and the woman asked the man why he did it, why he went walking in the countryside if the countryside were such an inhospitable environment for him.

"Oh, sometimes, I like to see how the other half live; to leave my comfort zone, so to speak."

The woman nodded with interest: she always enjoyed hearing people's reasons for coming to the countryside and then comparing those reasons with her own. Her own reasons were prosaic: she simply adored fresh air, open spaces, and good wholesome exercise. She, indeed, looked the part, every inch the woman of the country, whereas her new friend looked like a city-dweller trying too hard to look like a man of the shires.

"Feel free to walk with me," the woman said.

Another joke sprang to the man's mind, this one even lamer than was his last. "We can ramble together," he quipped, before grinning with satisfaction at the sheer genius of his comic gift.

"I came out here for solitude," the woman said, "but solitude's not much fun on one's own." She looked even more proud of her witticism than the man had been of his.

"Indeed, it isn't," the man replied.

"What's your name?"

"Francis," the man said, "but please don't ever call me Frank."

"My name's Stephanie, but please don't ever call me Steph."

"It's a deal."

As he followed the couple, Oswald felt oppressed by what was exciting Stephanie: fresh air, open spaces, and good wholesome exercise. Oppressed, not because what he was experiencing for the first time was disagreeable to him, but simply because he was experiencing it for the first time. He had no idea where he was; and still less idea what was around him. He was a man not only out of place but also out of time.

To him, the dialogue of the couple was stilted: though they spoke his language, it was a strangely not-quite-familiar version of it that he heard as he followed the man and the woman along the public footpath and listened to them.

The conversation ceased when they arrived at another pub; Oswald watched the man and the woman as they regarded the ivy-clad building as if they had just stumbled across the eighth wonder of the world; with reckless smiles, that was, and eyes bulging like oversized marbles in their sockets.

Oswald followed them into the public house and stepped back into the old lady's living-room.

Again, he squinted, this time as his eyes adjusted to the darkness, and for a while he was seeing visions of the other place, with its bright light and lavish colours; its vibrant greens and blues, especially; all of which were imprinted on his mind's eye, indelible images that would haunt him for the rest of his life.

"Are you all right?" the old lady asked. "You look like you've seen a ghost."

"I'm fine," Oswald said with all the diffidence of a schoolboy greeting his parents at the breakfast table. "I just felt a little queer for a moment, that's all." He took the tablecloth to the old lady and handed it to her.

"Thank you, son," the old lady said.

"May I ask you something?" Oswald had asked the question nervously; and he awaited the reply with some trepidation as he could not help but feel that he had spoken out of turn.

"Of course, son, go ahead and ask."

"Is your name Stephanie?"

The old lady peered into the distance vacantly for a moment, her mind searching for any association in her past with the name Stephanie. It was her turn now to look haunted.

"You know," she said, "I really don't know."

"Do you know a man named Francis?"

"No, son, I don't think I do."

Earlier that day, at the old man's house, the very same scenario, from entering the house to the present conversation, had unfolded …

"May I ask you something?"

"Of course, son, go ahead and ask."

"Is your name Francis?"

"You know, I really don't know."

"Do you know a woman named Stephanie?"

"No, son, I don't think I do."

"Lay the tablecloth on the table by the window, would you, son," the old lady said, as the old man had said, "and I'll see to the tea."

"How was the old lady?"

Oswald and Sonia were back in the café drinking coffee.

"Same as always …"

"And the old man?"

"Likewise…"

"You looked terrible this morning, Oswald, and you look even worse now."

"Reality's a nightmare, and my reality is worse than my nightmares."

"You had a nightmare last night?"

Oswald nodded sadly.

"Do you want to tell me about these nightmares?"

"Not really…"

"It might help."

"I had several dreams," Oswald sighed. "The first of them was more like a sleeping recollection."

"What do you mean?"

"It was like it actually happened."

"Dreams are powerful things."

"No, I mean it was like it happened, way back, and I was simply recalling the events in my dream."

"You have no memory of the event?"

Oswald shook his head, sadly, anguished once more by his inability to recall the past at will.

"Tell me what happened."

"It was a time when there was light, you know, *real* light. For several days, I kept going to an art shop to look at canvasses and brushes, because I was thinking about taking up art, and this girl—well, a young woman, of my age—served me and advised me about what I should buy. I bought some things, based upon her advice, but I kept returning to the shop, on the pretext of wanting to buy more things, just so I could see her. She'd told me that she was a sculptress. So, one day, I wrote a poem, called it *The Sculptress*, took it to the shop, and gave it to her. Then I left the shop, too shy to speak with her. I went back to the shop a couple of hours later and she refused to serve me. She refused even to talk to me. Then she grabbed her coat and left the shop in a hurry. I ran after her. I didn't know her name, but I called after her. She continued to run, and I carried on running after her. Then she ran into the road—she was *that* desperate to get away from me—and was hit, first by a bus, then by a car going one way, and then by a car going the other way. She was so beautiful. But the last I saw of her was broken bones, a smashed skull, and brains and guts all over the road. It could have been love. Instead, it was carnage."

"And you think that actually happened?"

Oswald nodded.

"To you?"

He nodded again, so that his head started to ache with all the nodding.

"And to *her*," he said.

"That's terrible."

Oswald risked another up-and-down movement of his head.

"Then I had a dream about you," he said.

"Me?"

"We were married. You were my wife. Those two words again: 'married' and 'wife'. And I was your husband."

"'Husband?' What a strange word that is."

"You went to visit someone for a few days, but you were gone for weeks, so I went looking for you. I thought you might be dead. But you were there. We were sitting in your friend's living-room, drinking tea, when into the room came another one of you, a replica. So, instead of not finding you there at all, I found two of you. And you—both of you—and your friend acted as if there being two of you were totally normal. I was spooked. Then I woke up and there you were, lying beside me. It had been a bad dream, that's all. I turned over onto my other side, and there you were, again. I was lying between two of you. Again, I was spooked. Then, again, I woke up, this time for real. It had been a dream within a dream. My head ached like hell when I woke up."

"I'm not surprised."

"I had another dream. I dreamt that you fell from a high place."

"A high place?"

"We were living in a flat, many storeys above the ground. You were cleaning the outside of the windows, but you leaned out too far, and fell. I heard only a whelp of anguish as you fell, and my heart sank, it ached, and I got ready to jump after you, so that we would die together. Then I woke up. It was the middle of the night. I was sweating. I was scared. Though I was relieved when I realised that it was just a dream."

"So, the dream about my falling came before the dream within a dream?"

"Yes, the 'two of you' dreams came just before I woke up and had to get up."

"My dreams, too, are weird, though I don't remember anything about any of them, except that they're weird."

Suddenly, piercing the hum of general chatter pervading the café, and the clinking of cutlery and crockery, Oswald exclaimed, "I remember the name now!"

"Whose name?"

"The name of the friend you went to visit in my dream …"

"What was her name?"

"Adelia …"

"I don't know anyone named Adelia."

"Sonia!" It was Jim calling from behind the counter. "There's a phone call for you!"

"Who is it?"

"Someone by the name of Adelia!"

Oswald and Sonia looked at each other as if they were falling together from a great height and were only a moment away from hitting the ground.

Blogger

Allan Wood (known to his friends as Woody Allen) sat in his usual place, in his usual lunchtime haunt, Davie's Dishes, a traditional British greasy spoon, in the High Street, owned and managed by Davie Dish, a handsome fellow known to the women in the town as Dishy Dave.

His place in the corner of the café was reserved for him by the proprietor and every weekday lunchtime he sat there, at the table for two, eating his lunch, drinking his tea, and reading his tabloid newspaper.

Often, he had a surly young man for company, for Colin Crimpton would sit opposite him whenever he was in the café and there was nowhere else to sit.

Colin was there that day and he watched Allan eat his steak-and-kidney pie and chips as if eating pie and chips were some kind of esoteric ritual. He was fascinated by the way that Allan hunched over his food as he ate and read his newspaper at the same time, not looking at his food as he speared it with his fork and raised it to his mouth.

Allan sensed that Colin was building himself up to launch his opening broadside of the day, and he braced himself for the usual ridiculous question.

"What are you reading, Allan?"

"The newspaper," Allan replied without moving his head by so much as an inch.

"I can see that."

"So why did you ask?"

"I meant, what are you reading about in the newspaper?"

"I'm reading about a boy whose dad had a sex-change and became his mum, and whose mum had a sex-change and became his dad. Needless to say, the poor kid's a bit confused."

"Well, yes, I suppose he would be."

Jenny, the waitress, delivered Colin's bacon butty and mug of tea and said what she said to all the customers when giving them their orders: "Tuck in!" It was her catchphrase. It goes without saying that often she had to listen to wisecracks from the punters, such as, "You can tuck me in anytime, darling."

Colin bit a chunk out of his bacon butty and slurped some tea.

"Who's on page three today?" he asked once he was in the eating and drinking groove.

"They did away with the Page Three Girl, more's the pity," Allan replied.

"Yes, well, they *were* on dodgy ground with that."

"Were they?"

"They extolled family values and plastered naked women all over page three."

"So?"

"Can't you see the conflict there?"

"Not really…"

"So, it was a case of tits and arse for all the family, was it?"

"It was hardly pornographic."

"May I confide in you, Allan?" Colin had had his say on the matter and was keen to change the subject.

"If you must…"

"I'm in trouble."

"You? In trouble? What have you been doing now? Sticking fireworks up ducks' arses again?"

"That was when I was a kid. You know that. And it's 'rectum'."

"I bet you wrecked 'em! You must have blown 'em to bits!"

Colin shook his head as if to shake Allan's childish words out of his mind, and then he leaned across the table, confidentially, lest any eavesdroppers should hear.

"I'm in trouble with the law, Allan," he said under his voice.

"I always thought you would come to a sticky end."

"The thing is I'm innocent, totally innocent."

"That's what they all say."

"Let me tell you what happened…"

Allan sighed. "Go on, then, but don't bend my ear."

"Today's Friday, right?"

"It is."

"Well, on Monday, I went to Sid's Café. I walked in and took a seat at a table in the corner. At the table next to mine was an attractive young lady. She looked at me as if I were some kind of weirdo. Anyway, since she'd arrived at the café long before me, she was on the verge of finishing her lunch. She finished it and left. The next day, Tuesday, I went to Jenny's Café, and there she was again. When she clocked me, her face went bright red, and she looked at me as if I were Jack the bloody Ripper. The next day, oh, my God, Allan, you wouldn't believe it! I went into Mick's Café, and who was the first person I saw as I entered? It was *her* again! This time, looking terrified, she left her food half-eaten, got to her feet, and left the café like a bat out of hell. Ten minutes later, a copper arrived at the café and told me that I was suspected of being a stalker and that, if I carried on stalking the girl, there would be consequences."

"You'd better stop stalking her then."

"I'm not stalking her!"

"So, it was just a coincidence that you followed the same woman into three different cafés three days running, was it?"

"Yes!"

"The police don't believe in coincidences."

"Do *you?*"

"Not when I'm eating my lunch …"

"This is a serious matter, Allan."

"Have the police charged you?"

"No …"

"There's no need to worry then …"

"If she'd been *here* when I arrived …"

"She *wasn't* here when you arrived, Colin, so stop fretting."

"I keep meaning to ask you, Allan: what do you do for a living?"

"I'm a sparky."

"An electrician?"

"Yes …"

"Right …"

"And you?" Allan sounded uninterested, as if he were just trying to be polite, and he had still to raise his head from out of his newspaper.

"I'm a blogger."

"What's a blogger?"

"Someone who writes blogs …"

"I'm none the wiser."

"I weave aphorisms into my blogs."

"Sounds painful …"

"Do you know what an aphorism is?"

"Isn't it some sort of stroke, in the brain?"

"That's an aneurism."

"It's all the same to me."

Colin whipped his phone out of his jacket pocket and tapped away at its screen in search of a website. Then he showed the screen to Allan. Since the text was so small, Allan peered at it myopically.

"'I could swim an ocean. It's just a notion.' What does that mean?"

"It's a play on words."

Colin played with his phone again and held out the screen to Allan.

"'In the pub, I talk about any subject from football to philosophy, but, after a few drinks, I find myself discussing anything from phootball to filosophy.' Is that wordplay too?"

"Yes, but of a different kind ..."

"It's all Greek to me."

"Here's another one."

"'Socialism is based on the principle that everyone needs dough, and capitalism on the principle that some knead it more than others.' I'm sure it's very clever, but I don't get it."

"Okay, how about this one?"

"'In the recent pub golf championship, the Whole Inn won, and not just some of the pub, either, but all of it.'"

Colin had watched tensely as Allan read the words, and now he waited expectantly for his companion's verdict.

"Well?"

"Again, it's clever, but way over my head."

Allan and Colin finished eating their food at the same time; both men pushed away their plates until they clashed in the middle of the table; both were now free to focus on their cups of tea and to continue their conversation unhindered by mouthfuls of food.

"You should check out my blog, Allan."

"I wouldn't understand a word of it."

"Today, I shall blog on the subject of retrospective necessitarianism."

"I haven't the faintest idea what that means, Colin."

"My blogs have several purposes, but the principal purpose is to make people think. Bertrand Russell once said: 'Most people would sooner die than think. And they do!' So, one of my themes is wordplay and the meaning of words and phrases, and I employ these to get people *used to* thinking. 'Do people care enough? Do enough people care?' I invite people to think if the two questions have the same meaning. Is 'The spring in Paris' the same as 'Paris in the spring'? I ask people if they know the difference between power and authority. Most people use the two words entirely interchangeably, but they have subtly different meanings."

"I *do* think, just not very deeply."

"Your mere *awareness* of that is a start, Allan."

"I take the world as I find it."

"There's a lot to be said for that, Allan, but some of us have to bear the burden of thinking for the masses."

"That's me all over: just one of the faceless masses."

"Some of what I write in my blogs is considered controversial, when all I'm doing is applying the rules of logic. For example, a few weeks ago, I wrote that there can be no diversity *between* countries if there is diversity *within* countries. In the comments, I got hammered for writing that, I was called an enemy of diversity, a fascist, all sorts, but, when I invited my critics to point out the logical flaw in my argument, they had no answer, other than again to call me a fascist.

"In another blog, I took issue with Samuel Johnson's claim that 'patriotism is the last refuge of the scoundrel'. I invited readers to ask themselves whether they had civic pride: that is, pride in their towns and cities, in terms of their heritage and governance. Then I asked readers if patriotism were not simply civic pride on a larger scale.

"Of course, lest anyone misunderstood what I was saying, I made it clear that I was talking about patriotism, not nationalism. But, even so, I then asked if nationalism were always and necessarily a bad thing. I stated categorically that it went without saying that the nationalism of, say, Adolf Hitler was a terrible thing. But what, I asked, of the nationalism of, say, Mahatma Gandhi?

"Nationalism is defined as the advocacy of or support for the political independence of a particular nation or people. India achieved its independence from Great Britain as a result of a nationalist movement, and nobody today would object to the foundation of the independent state of India, unless they are prepared to argue that Indians should have remained forever subjects of the British Empire."

Allan slurped some tea as he considered Colin's commentary, until it dawned on him that he had not a clue what his fellow diner was talking about.

"Needless to say, I got some stick for saying that too. This time, I was accused of being an apologist for imperialism, when, actually, I had argued *against* imperialism.

"That's why it is necessary for people like me to make people think about the words they use. For example, in a blog a few weeks ago, I wrote that, increasingly, the words 'sexism' and 'misogyny' are being conflated. All too often, men who make sexist comments, or who act in a sexist manner, are branded misogynists. Misogyny is the pathological hatred of women, and a man—or even a woman—might have perfectly good reason for hating women, ugly attitude though it be.

Sexism is merely the belief that women are innately inferior to men, which is a far cry from hating them.

"As you can imagine, I was accused of belittling women, and even of being a misogynist myself.

"Words must be used properly, Allan, or else they lose their meaning. Is that what people want: the degradation of our language?"

"I wouldn't know."

"The most controversial blog I've ever posted was the one about the mRNA vaccines during the pandemic."

"Don't talk to me about that bloody pandemic!"

"All I did was apply logic. The same people who say, 'My body, my choice,' when it comes to abortion—leaving aside the fact that the unborn child is *in* the body, not *of* the body—reject the same maxim when applied to the vaccine."

"I bet that went down well."

"It went down like a lead balloon. I was even accused of being a Catholic."

"*Are* you a Catholic?"

"Good God, no!"

"Right…"

"Then I argued that the same people who advocate gender self-identification reject the same principle when applied to the vaccine. Why, I asked, can't people self-identify as being vaccinated? Of course, that would be absurd. But so is gender self-identification."

"Do you like making trouble for yourself?"

"I was simply applying logic, a commodity in depressingly short supply in the world today. Of course, they hit back at me with the sex-gender distinction, a distinction that I find entirely spurious, but I replied that the point I was making concerned overturning objective, biological reality with subjective interpolations."

"Go easy on the big words, will you?"

"Okay, but you see what I'm driving at, don't you?"

"I think so."

"It's all about logic, as Bertrand Russell said."

"If you say so ..."

"Britain today has a shortage of mechanical engineers, Allan, and a surplus of social engineers."

"You could be right there."

"The country is so weak and defeatist."

"I can't argue with that."

Again, Colin thrust his phone in Allan's face and invited him to read what he saw.

"'Defeatism is corrosive and debilitating to the character at the moment when it passes from a reaction to a choice.' I'm not sure I follow that one."

"What I'm saying is that if people choose to be defeatist then they have lost before they have even begun."

"You're describing our useless football team ..."

"Think positive and you give yourself a chance of winning. Think negative and you've got no chance."

"I don't have much call for thinking, Colin. I leave thinking to people like your good self."

"In another blog, I wrote: 'One day, breathing will be a hate crime, and all the prisons will be full, but there will be neither prison governors nor prison officers, because they, too, will be prisoners, so, in effect, we shall all be free.'"

"There's a certain logic to that, I suppose."

"It's *pure* logic, Allan."

"I guess it is, yes."

"The other day, I wrote that, if people stopped posting their opinions on Facebook, Facebook would be saved the trouble of factchecking people's opinions with opinions of its own. I got hammered for that."

"It sounds like you get hammered for most things you write."

"I do, because I'm a controversialist, though I don't mean to be."

"I prefer to keep my head down. There's a lot to be said for a quiet life."

"My most persistent critic is a chap—well, it could be a woman, I suppose—with the username Freethinker. He's actually accused me of having a herd mentality. How can that be so when I'm constantly advocating freedom of speech? What he's saying is that, in promoting freedom of speech, I'm facilitating the expressions of ideas and opinions that he abhors; so, I must sympathise with those ideas and opinions; therefore, I *hold* those ideas and opinions. For him—or her—a freethinker is someone who agrees with him in matters socio-political. Anyone who disagrees is a fascist. It's mind-boggling, it really is. In his most recent response to my blog, he threatened to mobilise an army of freethinkers against me. I replied: 'You deride herd thinking, yet you talk about mobilising an army of freethinkers, and you cannot see the irony?'"

"What did he say to that?"

"I guess he's keeping his powder dry for his next assault."

"Well, you seem to enjoy the brickbats."

"The sad fact is that people like Freethinker actually think they're somehow liberal. Even if we were to take them at face value, we have to be mindful of the paradox of liberalism, which is that everything goes, let it all hang out, except illiberalism, the definition of which widens by the day. Liberalism today tolerates only a narrow spectrum of thought and expression. In an age of so-called tolerance, Allan, there is nothing more intolerant than a tolerant liberal."

"Perhaps these people are not liberals at all then?"

"They're *not*. But they *think* they are. They are Leftists, Cultural Marxists, call them what you will, herd thinkers par excellence, but they are in denial about that. It's tantamount to a mental illness. In fact, it *is* a mental illness. It's a mass derangement."

"I'd never thought of it like that."

"Leftists tie themselves up in knots with their twisted ideology, such as it is, Allan, because it's without solid foundations, but, rather, is an exercise in mindless iconoclasm. Challenge them and they are easily tripped up: they splutter, and bluster, and call you a fascist. Their worldview cannot bear even the gentlest scrutiny, for the simple reason that it has no internal logic. I have the utmost respect for any ideology, philosophy, whatever, as long as it's intellectually coherent. Theirs is not. Hence their anger when I take to it with a bit of logic. They fall right into my trap.

"For me, being broadminded—or openminded—is not about believing in everything and in nothing, it's about believing firmly in something but without closing my mind to other creeds and viewpoints."

"Except Leftism?"

"No, I'm perfectly happy for them to sell their wares in the marketplace of ideas, but they don't do me the same courtesy: they keep trying to shut down my stall. I challenge them only because they attack me in the comments section of my blog, day after day, though I admit that I do occasionally make the odd provocative post, just to see what reaction I get."

"Such as?"

"Oh, let me see…One time, I posted: 'I don't care what it's called! I call it Constantinople!' I was labelled an Islamophobe for that, and Freethinker reported me to the police. So much for freethinking!"

"You need to be careful, Colin, or you'll end up in the clink."

"Publish and be damned, Allan!"

"What?"

"Never mind…Look, on one level, what I do in my blog is harmless intellectual gymnastics, but, on another level, it's vital, it's a kind of crusade for commonsense values. Who would have thought that one day we would have to stand up for something so commonplace as common sense? Part of me thinks that the way to counter Cultural Marxism is not to challenge it, or to be affronted by it, but to laugh at it and watch on as it's slowly consumed by its own absurdity. But defending common sense has become imperative, since Cultural Marxists have taken over both the media and the educational establishment…and that joint takeover is feeding into the law."

"The law?"

"Consider the new Offences Against the Person bill going through parliament at the moment. It says that any offence against the person can be deemed a hate crime if the victim of the offence *perceives* it to be a hate crime. So, if you were to mug a Jewish man in the street, and the victim said that, to his mind, your principal motive for mugging him was his Jewishness, rather than the simple wish to deprive him of any property on his person, that offence would have to be treated by the police as a hate crime and not a robbery."

"How would I know that the guy was Jewish?"

"You wouldn't! And that's my point! Of course, you would know if a man were of African or Asian origin, but you would still mug that man because you wanted his money, not because of the colour of his skin. But, under this new law, your offence would be considered not racially *aggravated*, but racially *motivated*, if the victim were to deem it so."

"Like you say, though, my victim would have to call it a hate crime."

"What would be the chances of your offence, in such a case, *not* being deemed racially motivated, Allan? You wouldn't stand a chance. I'm all for inclusiveness, and for some proportionate correction of historical injustices—not *perceived* but *actual* injustices—but this is not the way to do it. It is indicative of a society turning in on itself and, in so doing, throwing logic and common sense out of the window. It's a crying shame. The saddest thing about it is that only a tiny number of Members of Parliament have made the stand for logic and common sense, when debating the bill, and they have been dismissed as cranks and mavericks, at best, or, at worst, fascists. The small number of sane people left in this world are now considered crazy. If there were only one sane person left in a world gone mad, that person would be considered the crazy one."

"Now you're talking about something I *can* understand, Colin. I do feel that something is not quite right about the world today. It's moving in a disturbing direction."

"Indeed, Allan! Eccentricity is the last bastion of individuality, yet both are loathed by the woke mob, for the simple reason that freethinking leads inevitably to people exercising common sense and so exposing the pernicious absurdity of Leftist thinking."

"Why are you laughing?"

"Well, on a less serious note, when it comes to individuality and eccentricity…Okay, I went up to Teesside to visit my sister last week. Whilst she was out shopping, her husband planted a palm tree in the front garden. It was meant to be a pleasant surprise for my sister. When she got home and saw the tree, her husband said, 'Well, what do you think?' 'It looks ridiculous, Eric,' she said. 'What's ridiculous about it?' Eric said. 'It's a bloody palm tree!' my sister said. 'In Middlesbrough!'"

Allan laughed. "And what did *you* think of the palm tree in Middlesbrough?"

"My sister was right. It looked ridiculous. But why not a palm tree in Middlesbrough? It's not as if Middlesbrough couldn't do with brightening up a bit."

"I've never been to Middlesbrough, but I've heard that it's rather grim."

What followed happened so quickly that nobody involved in the incident realised what was happening.

The doorbell of the café chimed as another customer entered, but the only person who noticed the newcomer was Colin Crimpton, who, without quite knowing why, looked over his shoulder to apprehend the pretty young woman.

He saw her before she saw him.

"Oh, my God!" he exclaimed. "It's her!"

That is when she saw him.

In panic, she fled; she ran out onto the street, turned left, and ran for her life; to her disbelief, she saw that she was being pursued with gusto by her stalker.

"Stop!" Colin yelled as he continued his chase. "We need to talk!"

A police officer came out of nowhere, planted himself in front of Colin, and intercepted him.

"Oh, it's you!" the policeman said. "Up to your old tricks again, are you?" He peered into the distance and beheld the fleeing young woman. "Yes, she's the one who complained about you."

"You don't understand!" Colin protested. "Let me explain!"

Suddenly, a familiar face appeared on the scene.

"Allan!" Colin pleaded. "Tell the officer what happened!"

Allan watched as Colin was bundled into a police car and driven away. He had never understood Colin's strange world. What Colin talked about was a mystery to him. He did not understand what was happening to Colin now. He wanted simply to keep to the world that he knew and understood. There was a world that was familiar to him. That is where he belonged. That is where he would stay.

Churchgate

Dennis McSwain was not a simple man, far from it, but he wished only to live a simple life, teaching history at a decent secondary school, in a pleasant provincial market town, and submitting himself to the rigours—the rewards, too—of a way of life rooted in faith. He enjoyed his home, a modest apartment in a quiet street, embellished as it was with the finest art and books and music. A wife would have been a bonus, children an added bonus. At forty-two, time was running out for him to be a father, he felt, though he remained eminently eligible a bachelor.

Marriage, though, he thought to himself as he made his way along the rain-soaked street: who is there for me to marry in this town? The women here are either married, or too old, or too young, or divorced and cynical, or just plain unsuitable.

In the latter category—in fact, she was covered by three of the aforesaid categories—was Janice, the woman whom he had condescended to date the previous evening. She was the chalk to his cheese and, as such, he would not be seeing her again unless she saw him first. She was a pleasant enough person; her conversation, however, had made his head spin with the sheer banality of it all, her focus having been on a near-relentless comparison of the prices of various groceries in various supermarkets. Then there was her laugh: it was a noise not unlike that of a cat being strangled, and it had attracted the attention of other drinkers in the bar. The screeching and wailing, which together had formed the highly distinctive laugh, had all the social impact of a meat-cleaver at a vegetarians' convention, and it would have made it difficult, if not impossible, to take her anywhere. The kind of noise she might have made when making love, he could only imagine, and he rebuked his imagination for persistently bringing it to mind.

Her varicose veins were not exactly attractive, either, and he recalled how he had become acquainted with them during the evening, as she crossed this leg over the other, and the other leg over this, back and forth, to reveal two mini-replicas of the Ganges Delta around her ankles.

After the drinks, and against his better judgement, he had invited her back to his place for a nightcap, whereupon she had provided further evidence—as had he—of a fundamental incompatibility between them.

As he was preparing the drinks, then, he had put on some music, before joining Janice, who sat in the middle of the sofa, intentionally, it had seemed to him, leaving plenty of space beside her for him, and enough space either side of each of them for a seamless transition from the upright to the horizontal, should the evening take such a turn. Alas, for Janice, he had parked himself in the armchair, a safe distance away from the sofa.

Janice had made a face, and pricked an ear, to indicate that she was savouring the music.

"I love a bit of Beethoven," she had said.

"This isn't Beethoven," Dennis had replied.

"Beethoven's Fifth and Sixth Symphonies are wonderful," she had blundered on, surprising Dennis for knowing the first thing about the great composer's work, "but there's something truly special about his Ninth."

Dennis had sighed, incredulous that such an evening had befallen him.

"This must be symphony number ...Oh, damn and blast, what is it?"

"It's not Beethoven!" Dennis had exclaimed, his patience spent by this point.

"What?" Janice had replied in kind.

"We're not listening to Beethoven," Dennis had declared impatiently.

"No?" Janice had said.

"No!" Dennis had answered.

"What *are* we listening to then?" the flustered Janice had asked.

"Rossini," Dennis had said. "He's about as far removed from Beethoven as you can get."

"Oh," Janice had whimpered.

"Do you like Rossini?" Dennis had enquired, the question more rhetorical than real, since it was as clear as day that the woman knew not the first thing about the Italian composer and his work.

"Oh, yes," Janice had replied. "It goes down a treat with ice and lemon."

The cackle had come in the wake of the gag, leaving Dennis to nurse the nagging feeling that he was having a bad dream from which wakefulness would soon deliver him.

Dennis was on his way to the twelve-fifteen Mass at his local church, and he realised that he had just enough time to pop into the dental clinic to make an appointment for a check-up. What he witnessed there disturbed him profoundly without quite surprising him.

When he arrived, a man was giving his details to the receptionist.

"Surname, please?" the woman on reception asked.

"Shakespeare," the man replied, "with an 'e'."

The young lady raised her eyebrows sceptically.

"First name?" she said.

"William …"

The receptionist rebuked him with her eyes for wasting her time.

"Look," the man responded, "my parents have a wicked sense of humour, okay?"

The woman sighed her irritation.

"Address?" she went on.

"Thirteen Hamlet Way…"

The young lady was by now struggling to contain her exasperation.

"Date of birth?" she said.

"Sixth of January, nineteen-ninety," the man replied. "Yes, I know, it's the twelfth night…of Christmas. When my mother's waters broke, my parents had to drive to hospital in a storm. A tempest, you might say. It was all much ado about nothing for my Pee and Em. They're nothing if not stoical."

"Thank you, Mister Shakespeare," the receptionist said, trying to humour the man as if her life depended on it. "Doctor Marlowe will see you next Tuesday, at three o'clock."

"I have to be careful here with all these Shakespeare-related details of mine," the man said. "I don't want to get myself barred. Barred? Bard? Do you get it?"

The receptionist was having no more of the man's flannel.

"Thank you, Mister Shakespeare," she said with the calm resolution of the redoubtable schoolmistress.

After Dennis had made his appointment, with much less drama, he went back out onto the street relieved to be back in the sensible world, only to encounter, almost immediately, more madness.

As he was walking past the Orange Kipper, a hideous bar in which he, Dennis, would not have been seen dead, he beheld a young man of about twenty being launched out of the door and onto the street.

"This is a respectable establishment!" cried the man who had done the launching.

"Compared with what?" yelled back the man who had been launched. "Treblinka?"

"Don't you dare darken this door again!" the burly bouncer shouted back, before melting back into his fishy orange world.

The young man dusted himself down and staggered towards Dennis.

"What did you make of that little scene, then, mate?" he asked Dennis.

"I'd rather you didn't call me 'mate'," Dennis said in reply. "I must be at least twenty years your senior."

"Think nothing of it," the young man said. "I've got mates with twenty years on you."

Dennis stepped up the pace, but the young man, still unsteady on his feet, pursued him.

"My name's Hamish McNut," the young man announced, out of breath now with the effort of catching up with Dennis and then keeping up with him. "Friends call me Noddy because I've got such big ears. If you're wondering why I'm called Hamish McNut, but I haven't got a Scottish accent, well, there's a story there for you, my friend."

"Alas, I'm in too much of a hurry to hear it," Dennis said, hoping that he sounded firm enough to shake off the annoying young man, who, evidently, was either drunk or under the influence of drugs, or both.

"Okay," the young man said, "I'll tell you another story, a shorter one, instead."

"If you must," Dennis sighed as he endeavoured to put distance between himself and the young man.

"I was in Majorca last summer, and I bought an ice-cream, you know, as you do. It was sprinkled with that stuff. What do you call it? Hundreds and thousands? Anyway, never mind hundreds and thousands, it must have been narcotics, because I took a couple of bites out of that ice-cream and, man, as true as I'm chatting with you now, I started tripping like a Sunday afternoon in Clacton. Now, I'm the first to admit that I inhabit a strange universe, but even in *my* universe that was not meant to happen. I remember saying to myself, 'Jeez, this stuff's a bit different from the Mr Whippy you get back home!'"

"You couldn't make it up, could you?" Dennis felt that sarcasm was preferable to rudeness, though he was sorely tempted to tell the young man to get lost.

The young man then hailed a taxi, jumped in, and waved goodbye to Dennis with a theatrical flourish. Dennis was left hoping that that was enough lunacy in his life for one day, but that hope soon foundered on the treacherous rocks of harsh reality.

The next brush with insanity, then, came only a few minutes later, as he was walking past what appeared to be a new night club, an establishment every bit as garish and vulgar as the Orange Kipper. He was intercepted by another young man, this one apparently sober and not under the influence of drugs, though he turned out to be heavily under the influence of stupidity.

"Hi there, mate!" the young man said as he stepped in front of Dennis to block his path.

"Why does everyone keep calling me 'mate'?" Dennis muttered to himself.

"Want a voucher for Heaven?" The young man was calm and deliberate as he spoke, which for Dennis did at least make a refreshing change from his previous encounter with a youthful male, though the ensuing dialogue was wholly in keeping with the flavour of the day.

"Thanks, but I get my vouchers for heaven from the Catholic Church."

"Come again?"

"He *will*."

"Can we start again? Would you like a voucher for Heaven, my friend?"

"Sure, I'll take one."

"How old are you, my friend?"

"Forty-two …"

"Sorry, boss, you're too old."

"Is there an upper-age limit for entry into this club of yours then?"

"Well, no, gov, but forty-two … Well, that's a bit old for a nightclub, isn't it?"

"I would have thought that a club named Heaven would have quite a *high* upper-age limit."

"Sorry, mate, but I don't make the rules."

"What *are* the rules?"

"All I know is that, if I start handing out vouchers to blokes in their forties, my boss will be none too pleased."

"Who is your boss? Don Corleone?"

"His name's Sam Goldberg, actually. He's not a man you'd want to cross, if you know what I mean. He's a London man, new in town, branching out, like."

"This town's going to the dogs, so nothing surprises me anymore, not even London gangsters moving in and setting up dodgy nightclubs to serve as fronts for their money-laundering and drug-dealing."

"Are you a copper?"

"Do I look like a copper?"

"You could be undercover."

"Exciting as that sounds, I'm not."

"You should be careful what you say, mister."

"I know how your racket works, young man."

"You reckon? Well, I wish you a good day. Take it steady, my friend."

Having survived that little head-to-head, Dennis was soon being reacquainted with a madcap day hellbent on testing his patience to the limit. He was trying to turn his thoughts to matters more sublime—since he *was* on his way to church—but life, as was its wont, was right in his face, yapping and cajoling and taunting him, a constant irritant and unceasing menace.

At the next zebra-crossing, he saw a young woman (or an older girl, it was hard to tell) struggling to manoeuvre a pushchair down the kerb and into the road. He offered to help her.

"Don't be so bloody patronising!" the girl-woman replied. "I'm a woman, not a bloody invalid!"

Word for word, Dennis had received the same answer from a woman, two weeks before, when he had offered her his seat on a bus after he had noticed her struggling to stay on her feet during an especially bumpy ride. Then he had reflected that there can be no masculinity without chivalry and no femininity without graciousness.

Life, for all its madness and inherent evil, often taught him lessons that no amount of books could teach him, and at such instructive times he could almost be at peace with the world, or at least resigned to his place within it.

As he overtook the girl-woman, when crossing the road, he said to her, calmly and with a dignity worthy of the chivalry to which he had been called, "You might be a woman, but you're certainly no lady."

What she said in reply, mercifully for him, was lost in the din given by the bus waiting at the crossing, the impatient driver of which was revving the engine aggressively, as if he were irked by the constant need to stop his lumbering conveyance for the sake of lone men and teenaged girls and their ill-conceived progeny.

There were two vegan restaurants in the town and, weirdly, they were situated next to each other. One of them was called Bar Vegan, and the other Bar Vegas, so that not only the uncanny juxtaposition had passers-by scratching their heads in wonderment. A young man emerged from one of the establishments, and he was followed by another young man coming out of the other. Dennis studied the two men and wondered if they might not be twins. He wondered, too, if they were men at all.

"What the hell is happening to this town?" he said to himself. "Men with ponytails? Ripped jeans everywhere? I can't tell the difference between young men and young women anymore."

A man of about Dennis's age passed him in the street and, as he went, shouted at him: "I'm not a person anymore! I'm not even a number! I'm a bloody QR Code!"

As Dennis watched the man go by, he was overtaken by a curious hybrid emotion: a mixture of stark bemusement and profound kinship. The sense of kinship came from the feeling that his mind was at one with the stranger's, at least in terms of the matter in question, the bemusement from the perverse way in which the man had chosen to express himself. He feared that he himself might slowly become like these outlandish urban oddities and curiosities, contaminated, as it were, by their offbeat collective sensibilities.

He had completed the first of three parts on the journey from his flat to the church, the stage being marked (in his mind) by the presence of the town's main theatre, across the road and away to his right. It was an impressive edifice, for it had the appearance of an Ancient Greek temple, though for that it looked all the more incongruous amid the commonplace piles of brick and mortar dominating that quarter of the town.

The second part of the half-mile-long journey ran from the theatre to the market square, an enclave that was packed with fruit and vegetable stalls on Thursdays and Saturdays, and on every other day with speakers of all kinds, cranks and weirdos of all political persuasions and Christians of all denominations bar Catholic. He wondered what kind of oratorical gallery of the unhinged would greet him today, upon his arrival at the square, and he steeled himself for the spectacle.

He was not far into the second part of the journey when he was forced to invoke once again an interior monologue that he cared to banish from his consciousness, once and for all, but was never allowed to do so. The maniac on two wheels even had the audacity to ring his bell and demand that Dennis move out of the way, when Dennis was the one who was where he should have been, and was entitled to be, on the pavement, and the other breaking the law by trespassing on the pedestrian's domain.

"In this town, there is enough traffic to keep the humble pedestrian on his or her toes," the monologue began. "But this town has more than its fair share of what might be called cyclopaths. There are parts of the streets, havens of relative safety, where cars and buses cannot seek out pedestrians and exterminate them. Then there are the perennial corridors of uncertainty, avenues of peril, those elegant sidewalks and tranquil squares where nobody on foot can feel safe from the prospect of being wiped out by a lunatic on a bicycle."

"I'll get in the road, shall I?" Dennis hollered at the cyclist as he raced off to his terribly important destination for his terribly important meeting.

The cyclist replied with a raised middle finger, as if to say, "Swivel on that, you jerk!"

It was another uplifting moment for Dennis, another reason to celebrate the nobility of the human spirit, another reminder that the human race was set to enjoy a future as sunny and glorious as its past.

Whenever he walked to the church, which was practically every day, his thoughts became more sublime the closer he got to the church. He had noticed that about himself. It was as if the looming presence of the church, its very imminence, produced in his mind some kind of transfiguration of thought, a process of transition from the mundane to the godly via the pragmatic.

As it happened, at that moment, he remained mired in pragmatism, and his thoughts turned to his erstwhile fiancée, Florence, from whom he had separated, five years before, after a two-year engagement, after she left him to be with, and then marry, a man in London, a man reputed to be some kind of small-time gangster. She had taken her leave of the sheepfold and entered the lions' den. All the feelings that had assailed him after Florence's departure—sorrow, bitterness and disappointment, among them—had dissipated now, he had assimilated them to himself, so that he carried in his heart a heavy compound of emotions that might be termed disillusionment. The affair with Florence was not the first time that he had been unlucky in love; it did not represent his first engagement, either, for there had been two others. The sole consolation that he derived from Florence's betrayal was that she had taken up with a man who could not have been more different from himself, for that made it seem less personal and more of a lifestyle choice. He took what consolations in life that he could.

He was thinking about Florence because only the day before he thought he had seen her in the town centre. It had been a misty day, and the mist was only just starting to clear when the silhouette of a figure he knew all too well emerged from the earthbound cloud and then disappeared again, a mirage captured in grey and white, a ghost brushing against the corporeal world of which it was barely a part. It had been a fleeting glimpse, and of what exactly he was unsure. Had he really seen Florence? He decided that he had not, if only because he had not seen her in town in the five years since she left, so he thought it unlikely that he would start seeing her now. Moreover, the town was not Florence's hometown, she had no friends and family there, so why would she come back, even for a daytrip, away from her exciting new life in the capital? She simply had no reason to be back in town.

Dennis recalled how he had felt when his fellow-Catholic Florence had left him and he had been made to realise that she had been plotting her departure for weeks, if not months, her heart set on another man.

He kept returning to the word "trust"; to the very idea of trust, indeed.

Trust is precious, he reflected. To trust someone, and to be trusted by them, is a precious gift; it is something to treasure. Florence should reflect on the sacrifices she has made to her trustworthiness and integrity to get where she is now, having rejected a simple, pious life in favour of something more lively, edgy, and dangerous. She is being looked after, all her material needs catered for, and that is all that matters to her. She has her own small portion of paradise. But she ought to have known that she cannot sin her way into paradise, not even to some earthly approximation of it.

That is what he was saying to himself at that moment.

He remembered what he had told himself, time after time, during the dark days after Florence had gone. He recalled the words verbatim now.

"I feel so low. I feel as if someone spent months plotting my murder, and then plunged the knife into my back, killing me, and that I, though dead, have somehow lived to suffer the aftermath of my murder. Yes, I can offer up my pain to the Lord, but the sense of betrayal is so heavy, it is palpable, it's like a deadweight that I carry around with me all the time. I invested so much of my trust in you, Florence, after you gave me your 'solemn promise' that you would marry me; after you had told me: 'Trust me and you will not be disappointed.' Why had you felt the need at the time to tell me that? Were you not quite able to trust yourself? You were my Eternal Kiss and I your Eternal Treasure. People look after their treasure. That's why it's called treasure: it is to be treasured.

"After all that has been said and done, however, I feel more pain about what you've done to *yourself* than about anything you've ever done to *me*.

"When you left me, you said that you would pray for me; and I replied that *you* needed *my* prayers more than *I* needed *yours*.

"I stand by that statement even now."

He walked on, and on, and the world left him in peace, so that nothing and nobody came between him and his thoughts.

For Dennis, thoughts always led to ideas, and he loved ideas almost as much as he despised opinions: an opinion is to an idea what the earth is to the sun, or what Man is to God. That was an idea of his, not an opinion. An idea illuminates, it shines light upon the world, but its fate, all too often, is to fall so far from grace that eventually it is reduced to the state of a humble opinion. Thus does an idea descend from the sunlit uplands of philosophy to the clamorous flatlands of politics, and from the City of God to the grubby, over-crowded marketplace of Mammon.

He was nearly at the market square, and, because that day was not a market day, he was expecting the usual rogues' gallery of political cranks and religious fruitcakes, expounding on this and expostulating on that, which, together, would form a cacophony of discordant sound fit to be ignored by all but the warped and the curious.

The words of the priest, Father Daniel O'Meara, came back to him as he approached the square, the words that he had heard on BBC Radio 4 that morning, on the programme *Moving The Spirit*.

"The first reading at Mass today is from the Book of Genesis. It describes Jacob's dream of the ladder stretching up to heaven, with the angels of God ascending and descending. When he awoke, Jacob exclaimed: 'How awesome is this place! This is nothing less than the house of God! This is the gate of heaven!'

"We should have the same awestruck reverence when entering our churches, which are places where the Lord is present more really than at Bethel. Our tabernacles are the house of God. The sacrifice of the Mass is the ladder that reaches up to heaven. The angels congregate above our altars in adoration and wonder.

"On a more grounded level, the architect Sir Ninian Comper wrote: 'A church should pray of itself with its architecture. It is its own prayer, and it should bring you to your knees when you enter.'"

Dennis laughed to himself, for the first thought that occurred to him whenever he entered his church was how to keep warm during the Mass, even in summer.

He was trying to block out the noise of the market square now by focussing on the Mass and his imminent arrival at the church. He was reflecting yet again.

A week or so ago, then, a colleague had said to him: "Why do you do it, you Catholics? Why do you go to cold, draughty buildings, get on your knees, face a block of stone, and invoke a being that does not exist?"

In reply, Dennis might have invoked Saint Thomas Aquinas: "To one who has faith, no explanation is needed. To one without faith, no explanation is possible."

He might have hit back with the words of Saint Paul: "Now faith is the substance of things hoped for, the evidence of things not seen."

Alas, all that had come out of his mouth was a feeble: "Cold, draughty buildings? On the contrary, my friend, most Catholic churches nowadays are perfectly adequately heated."

He laughed at that as he walked past a man standing on a soapbox proclaiming that the world was poised "between the times", since "Christ's victory is assured but not yet complete".

The man offered Dennis some leaflets containing information about the Pentecostal Church.

"I'm a Catholic," Dennis told the man, tartly, and he declined to take a leaflet.

"The denomination is not important," the man replied. He clutched at his heart as he added, "It's what's in here that counts."

"Oh, you'll find that the denomination is *all* important," Dennis said as he left the preacher in his wake, a preacher momentarily dumbstruck and unable to preach.

His ears were being battered by all kinds of noise from all kinds of speakers, and he did not trouble himself with establishing what any of the speakers were saying, or whereabouts on the politico-religious spectrum they were standing when they spoke.

He heard from somewhere close to him a prospective speaker being introduced in gushing terms by a drooling acolyte: apparently, the would-be declaimer was "marvellous", "fantastic" and "wonderful", and her words "powerful". Dennis did not hang around long enough to find out if the speaker was worthy of so many superlatives as he was in a hurry to get to Mass on time. Even the few souls who were standing and watching the performance of the "spellbinding" orator (as they had been told he would be) were doing so more out of curiosity than a genuine wish to submit their ears to a dashing, persuasive oratory. The little of the speech that Dennis heard was devoid of substance, the thrust of it being to denounce "the system" and in words that were harsh and condemnatory, not to mention personal, for the people who kept "the system" running were "capitalist stooges" whose "days were numbered".

Dennis reflected that the more superlatives there were in a speech the emptier was the rhetoric, as if the barrage of compliments was designed to conceal the hollowness of the message.

That thought unfolded into another: the ease with which blind loyalty inherent in tribalism (my side good, your side bad) trumps notions of intrinsic right and wrong shows how little the human race has advanced since the Enlightenment. He was thinking of tribalism of the political kind, but he knew that the idea applied to tribalism of any kind.

Tribalism, he believed, was essentially selfish, for it looked inwards, rather than outwards, and it was sympathetic with the impulse within the individual that would seek mercy for oneself but justice for others. "And what of those iconoclasts and deconstructionists?" he asked himself. "They would pick apart the fabric of society, and pull down its pillars, and offer no ideas as to what might be put in their places."

Before he left the market square, he turned on his heels and saw a mass of people, most of whom missed the point entirely and wasted a lot of energy in doing so.

He saw, too, that most of the people cheering and clapping the speakers were recording proceedings on their phones. Gil

Scott-Heron, famously, had said that "the revolution will not be televised". He was not wrong, Dennis thought, for the revolution will be filmed by the revolutionaries themselves on their smartphones.

There was no compassion in what he was witnessing: even the Christian preacher was foaming at the mouth with righteous indignation, threatening people with hellfire and damnation, urging people to offend each other into heaven rather than to flatter each other into hell.

It was all so self-serving, so self-aggrandising, so "look at me".

He cast his mind back to the previous week, when he had given an impromptu homily in the parish centre after the Sunday Mass. It had been occasioned by the discussion about the priest's sermon that had broken out, as discussions always broke out about the priest's sermon in the parish centre after the Sunday Mass. The words he had spoken on that day had come from his own writings, and they had come out exactly as he had written them, which had puzzled some among his audience, even those familiar with his academic style of thinking and his precise and measured way of speaking.

"Every war, every battle, every conflict, every argument, every unkind thought or word or deed, every act of cruelty, every act of indifference, every decision to put compassion aside for the sake of self, each and every one of these actions is a tragedy for the human race. They diminish us all, and the smallest of these abominations leads, inexorably and ineluctably, to the greatest.

"In our greatest weakness are the seeds of our greatest strength. Our greatest strength exhorts us never to allow it to become our greatest, besetting weakness. Strength and weakness, far from being at odds, the one with the other, are mutual guardians of the soul, and each one must guard the other, even as it guards the soul."

The thought kept coming back to him: had he really seen Florence on the previous day? Well, he considered, the country was now being run by fascists, in the form of the British Social Movement, and the cabinet contained one Nathalie Front (from Burnley) and one Brittany Power (from Basildon), so anything, anything in the world, was possible.

The market square in that town had always been a veritable microcosm of the country at large; a mass of contradictions; a bastion of tradition and yet a barometer of change; Middle England, now trying to hold the centre, yet flying to the extremes, going off on several tangents whilst busily falling in upon itself.

The church was in sight now, and so his thoughts became embalmed, soothed by his proximity to the city atop the hill, the light on the lampstand that could be hidden by no bushel.

Thoughts of the afterlife came to him.

About heaven there was one thing he was certain: that on our day of personal judgement, when we stand before the Almighty, we will see ourselves as God sees us. That certainty alone should be enough to make any God-fearing person mend their ways, and not only that but also to purify their hearts and minds for the sake of their souls.

The shepherd children at Fatima had been shown by Our Lady that hell exists: they had seen a vision of the souls in hell, no less terrifying for being momentary, and it had impressed upon them the unbearable sufferings and torments of the souls lost to hell forever.

To Dennis' rational mind, the visions at Fatima affirmed the existence of hell, though what the children had seen, courtesy of Our Lady, was a reality displayed in terms that they could understand, thereby enabling them to communicate what they had been shown, and to be understood by the great mass of humanity incapable of thinking in abstract terms.

He did not think for a second that hell existed exactly as the children of Fatima had seen it. Our Lady had simply wanted to warn humanity not to suppose that hell was merely a place of the medieval imagination, but a real place, a place to be feared. He knew that hell existed. He knew, too, that purgatory existed. He was in no doubt about that, for the simple reason that the Church had told him that it existed, and that was all the evidence he needed. His greatest doubt was the existence of this earthly plane, Greene's "ravaged and disputed territory between the two eternities", because it often seemed a place where experience was more speculative and less concrete than any anticipated experience in any realm associated with the afterlife. He felt that way now: disconnected from a reality that was constantly shifting, touchable, but always just out of reach.

For Dennis, heaven and hell were simply different realms from the experienced material world or physical universe. Heaven, for him, then, was simply a realm in which the soul was in permanent and everlasting communion with God; it was an eternal, spiritual Eucharistic feast, not parallel with the material world but immanent, coextensive with it, but also going beyond it in time if not in space. Hell was the same except that it was a realm eternally cut off from God, from communion with Him, and agonisingly so.

Heaven is a realm where the soul is in eternal communion with its lived earthly life, but as a spiritual distillation of all that was good about it. Every second, every episode, every event, every thought, word and deed in which good had been contained, all that goodness, and only that goodness, can be apprehended in the heavenly realm. Heaven is a place where the soul is in communion with the good only, for the good is God, and God is good. Pure goodness is from God, and God is pure goodness itself.

Heaven, to adapt Iris Murdoch's formula, is the Sovereignty of Good.

As for hell, for "good" read "bad", or just plain "evil".

Purgatory is a realm where souls are in communion with God, and therefore with their own personal, earthly good, but also, through God, with their own personal, earthly evil, which will be purged, slowly but surely, to facilitate their eventual entry into heaven.

Dennis was confident that there was no hint of heresy in such thinking, for the Church no longer clung to the idea of heaven as being somewhere "up there", and hell as being a place "down there", with its attendant medieval imagery.

Heaven, hell, and purgatory: these are realms of communion. The key word, then, is "communion". As in life, so in death: communion is the watchword, the be all and end all.

Dennis went up the steps to the church and, just before entering, he turned on his heels and looked down at the noisy, clamorous market square, with its speakers and its protesters and its preachers. The country—the world, no less—really had taken a turn for the worse, and he tried to trace a thread back to the source of the trouble, to see where it had all started to go wrong. That was a mental effort that he would save for another time, for now he was focussed on the Holy Mass and giving the Almighty something like the attention He deserved.

Into the church he went. He dipped a finger in the stoop and crossed himself with holy water. He genuflected. He took his usual place three pews from the front, on the right of the church. He fell to his knees. He put his hands together and said, "Lord, let me die to sin, lest I die in hell," paraphrasing Saint Augustine.

As he sat up and waited for the Mass to start, he looked around the church and marvelled at its beauty, a beauty that made the sheer agony of spending an hour in the church's pews all the more incongruous. For him, being in that church was like eating a chocolate gateau whilst having his testicles squeezed. The church was opulent, but there was something decidedly penitential about its pews, for they defied any attempt at getting comfortable, either sitting or kneeling. He always left the church spiritually refreshed but feeling like he had just spent a night sleeping in a wardrobe.

He was fully engaged in the Mass, but only until just after he had taken communion and he was walking back to his pew, for it was then that he saw her, Florence, standing in the queue for communion. He stopped in his tracks so suddenly that the woman behind him walked into the back of him like a car shunting into the back of the car in front after an abrupt halt. He apologised to the woman, but his eyes remained fixed on his quarry as he stumbled back to his place. There she was, Florence, there was no doubt about it. Though she had been gone only five years, he had expected her to look different somehow, even in some small way, but she had not changed in the slightest, save for her sporting a jacket that he had not seen her wearing before. Her black hair still cascaded down her back like waters of ebony in freefall; she still walked perfectly upright, cocooned in her own dignity and lofty detachment; and, as she received the host on her tongue, she still stood elegantly, her feet close together, a lady in full possession of herself, body and soul.

Dennis said to himself: "She's back. I cannot deny the evidence of my own eyes. But what am I going to do about it? What, indeed, *should* I do about it?"

When the Mass was over, he waited for Florence to get up and leave, so he could follow her out onto the street and talk with her. He waited, and he waited, until he and Florence were the last two people left in the church. She appeared not to have seen him from her pew on the other side of the church, level with his.

He called over to her in a raised whisper: "Florence!"

The woman remained impassive, not statuesque exactly, but moving only her eyes to blink and her chest to breathe.

"Florence!" he called again.

He was met with the same response.

Eventually, the woman he thought was Florence took her leave of the pew, genuflected gracefully, and then floated out of the church like the summer haze dissipating in the slowly encroaching heat of the morning sun.

As he followed her out of the church, slowly, jumbled words of all kinds jostled in his mind for his attention, but he was powerless to make of them anything resembling coherence. What was he going to say to her, if and when he caught up with her? Though he was a reticent man, he was never tongue-tied: he always had words for every occasion, even—especially—when they had to be conjured without preparation. Words came to him easily, and almost always the right ones.

He found her waiting for him at the foot of the steps like an actress at the theatre waiting in the wings for her cue.

"Florence?" he said, blinking as his eyes adjusted to the light after the dimness of the church.

"Hello, Dennis…"

"You're back."

"You're as observant as ever."

"What are you doing back in town?"

"That remains to be seen."

"I thought I saw you yesterday."

"It seems that you *did* see me."

"Are you back for good?"

"That depends…"

"On what?"

"Let's walk."

"Do you want to go somewhere?"

"On the way to church, I passed a café I hadn't seen before. It must be new. The Liberty Café. Do you know it?"

"I know it well."

"What's it like?"

"Well, the pâté de foie gras there leaves a lot to be desired, but I can recommend the bacon butty."

"I've missed your humour, Dennis, I have to say."

They walked awhile in silence, neither knowing what to say. The café was situated to the east of the market square, so they were able to avoid the noise and the dirt and the multitude of speakers. They had almost arrived at their destination when Florence froze on the spot, startled. Dennis was alarmed by Florence's sudden change of demeanour: she looked terrified.

"It's him!"

"Who?"

"Sam…"

"Sam Goldberg?"

Florence looked at Dennis as if she had just seen the Archbishop of Canterbury riding on a donkey.

"You know him?" she said.

"I've heard of him."

"How?"

"He's the man you've been with these past five years?"

"Yes…"

"Isn't he some kind of gangster?"

Florence merely blinked sheepishly in reply.

"You left me for a gangster?"

Again, the blink…

"Florence!" the man exclaimed, as if he were greeting a friend he had not seen for a long time. "I thought I'd find you here!"

"This isn't your town, Sam," Florence responded defiantly. "Go back to London."

"You're coming back with me."

"I rather think that's Florence's decision to make, don't you?"

Sam shot Dennis with a look of contempt that suggested violence.

"Who the hell are you?" he spat.

"I used to be Florence's fiancé," Dennis replied.

"He's *still* my fiancé," Florence said. She turned her head to face Dennis. "If he wants to be."

"How cute are you two?" Sam sneered. He was the kind of man who could wish a child a happy birthday and still sound menacing. "I suppose you two have been cooking up this little reunion for weeks."

"Dennis had no idea I was back in town until he saw me in church an hour ago."

"No wonder you wouldn't marry me," Sam went on in a tone of voice that carried the implicit threat of violence in the future, should it be deemed necessary. "You were carrying a torch for this dude all along."

"I thank you for not pushing me into marriage, Sam. In that regard, you are a noble man."

Sam smiled at Dennis. "For five years, she made me live like a monk." He smiled again, this time with the cruelty of an April snow shower. "It's a good job I've got a few damsels in reserve, eh, you know, to help me keep my hand in and my end up."

"I might have known," Florence sighed.

"Well, what do you expect? Do I look like Saint Francis of Assisi?"

"Saint Francis of Assisi was all things unholy," Dennis ventured, not caring what Sam thought of his interjection, "yet God worked through him and made of him a saint."

Sam turned once more to Dennis.

"Florence, you need to teach this guy some manners," he growled, his eyes still boring into Dennis. "He keeps poking his nose where it's not wanted."

"Dennis can learn nothing from me, in terms of manners, still less from you."

"How very touching!"

"What do you want, Sam?"

"Why did you leave?"

"What you did to Lenny Mahoney was the last straw."

"Why are you worried about some jumped-up Paddy?"

"You knocked several of his teeth out."

"No, I didn't."

"The goons that work for you did, on your say-so, if you want to be pedantic."

"So? A dentist on the manor will get some much-needed work. I'll have boosted the local economy. I'm nothing if not community spirited."

"He's going to have you prosecuted."

Sam was pointing at Florence but looking at Dennis when he said, "She's on a roll today, this one." He laughed and reset his eyes on Florence. "He's going to prosecute me, is he? Lenny Mahoney wouldn't go near the law if his mother's life depended on it."

"I don't mean by the law. He has his own way of bringing people to justice. He won't mess about."

"Bring it on!"

"Lenny can afford new teeth, but you'll need more than a few new teeth by the time he's finished with you."

"You know so much about him, why don't you write his biography?"

"Five years with you taught me a thing or two about London's low life."

"You knew what you were getting yourself into. What did you expect? Choirs and angels? Discussions about Wittgenstein? You made your choice."

"And I'm making my choice now."

"I defended your honour. Why are you doing this?"

"My honour is not yours to defend."

"I saw the way Mahoney looked at you. He raped you with his eyes."

"I dare say he did. Have you never looked at a woman and undressed her in your mind?"

"Don't get smart with me, lady!"

"Goodbye, Sam!"

"I opened that nightclub for you! I even gave it a stupid religious name!"

"Give it to one of your floozies! And then rename it Hell!"

Sam ran his eyes over Dennis and Florence, who were now standing almost shoulder-to-shoulder in mutual solidarity. He knew that now was the time to execute a tactical withdrawal, so as not to compromise his dignity further. He knew that his absence would be more unsettling than his presence. His disappearance, following his withdrawal, would be ominous.

"You two will regret this little performance," he said at last.

Dennis and Florence watched as Sam melted into the crowd. It would be wrong to say that they were not afraid, but the sheer elation of being back together outweighed the fear, and it was an elation grounded in the knowledge that they now had more than their shared faith to bind them together, as if their shared faith were not enough.

Florence fumbled in her jacket pocket for something. She pulled out a ring and made to place it on her finger. "I kept it," she said. "May I?" she asked.

Dennis smiled the smile of a happy man. "You may."

They took each other's hand.

"I don't know about you," Florence said, "but I need something a tad stronger than a cup of coffee."

"So do I."

They wandered off together in search of a public house, their future together guaranteed. If their life together were a book, part two of two had just begun.

Little did they know, as they floated euphorically through the busy streets of the town, that Lenny Mahoney would soon ensure that never again would they have to fear the vengeful wrath of one Sam Goldberg.